THE FIVE ANCESTORS

鼠 Mouse

Jeff Stone

The Five Ancestors

THE FIVE ANCESTORS

鼠Mouse

Jeff Stone

Random House 🏠 New York

Visit us on the Web! www.randomhouse.com/kids

Educators and librarians, for a variety of teaching tools, visit us at www.randomhouse.com/teachers

www.fiveancestors.com

Library of Congress Cataloging-in-Publication Data
Stone, Jeff.
Mouse / Jeff Stone.—1st ed.
  p. cm.—(The five ancestors ; bk. 6)
Summary: In seventeenth-century China, orphaned ShaoShu, who can squeeze into small spaces, puts his life in danger when he becomes a spy for a young band of warrior monks known as the Five Ancestors and bravely infiltrates evil Tonglong's camp.
ISBN 978-0-375-83081-5 (trade) — ISBN 978-0-375-93081-2 (lib. bdg.) — ISBN 978-0-375-83082-2 (pbk.) — ISBN 978-0-375-89245-5 (e-book)
[1. Spies—Fiction. 2. Martial arts—Fiction. 3. Human-animal relationships—Fiction. 4. Orphans—Fiction. 5. China—History—1644–1795—Fiction.]
I. Title.
PZ7.S87783Mr 2009   [Fic]—dc22   2008034810

Printed in the United States of America
10 9 8 7 6 5 4 3 2
First Edition

for my agent, Laura Rennert

鼠Mouse

Jeff Stone

Henan Province, China
4348 – Year of the Tiger
(1650 AD)

CHAPTER
1

The Chinese junk pitched and rolled in the pounding surf, its ancient timbers groaning under the heavy load. The boat lay low in the water, cold spray blowing over its rails with each gust of the frigid autumn wind. Hidden below a tattered tarpaulin on deck, ShaoShu—Little Mouse—wondered what he'd gotten himself into.

He shivered. The damp sea air had soaked through his thin skin, deep into his tiny bones. He had only been aboard one day, but he already yearned to have his feet back on dry land.

ShaoShu had little experience on the water. True, he'd just spent more than a week traveling down the Grand Canal with his new friends, Hok and Ying, but that ride was nothing like this one. That was fun. This was agonizing. The sooner he was off this ship, the better.

The boat lurched suddenly on the choppy seas, and a wicked crosswind lifted one corner of the tarp. ShaoShu quickly snatched it back down, catching a glimpse of General Tonglong's long ponytail braid swaying just a few paces away. ShaoShu shuddered. Tonglong—the Mantis—was uncomfortably close.

As a homeless street urchin, ShaoShu had a lifetime of practice hiding in small, inconspicuous places. He had an unnatural ability to bend and twist his small body into all sorts of strange shapes, and he put these skills to use stowing away here on Tonglong's Chinese man-o-war in order to steal some information for his new friends. This, however, had been more than he'd bargained for. Perhaps he'd pushed his luck too far.

ShaoShu shifted his position ever so slightly, and he felt the weight of the shiny cylindrical object resting on his lap. It was nothing really, some sort of spyglass. While it might prove useful to him, he had mainly taken it because it was made of a highly polished brass and glimmered with a luster he couldn't resist. It was this same fascination with shiny objects that had brought him to his current hiding place.

With each passing wave, ShaoShu sank deeper into the largest pile of treasure he'd ever seen. He was surrounded by riches that even the Emperor would be hard-pressed to imagine: golden goblets, impossibly

intricate jade figurines, mounds of pearl jewelry—
all of it piled here on the boat's deck and covered
with a tarp like a worthless bale of straw. There were
other piles, too, though none as large or magnificent
as this one.

The treasure was connected to a series of dragon
scrolls that contained secret dragon-style kung fu
fighting techniques. One of the scrolls was also a map,
and Tonglong had used it first to find Ying's mother's
house, then to locate the treasure in a secret seaside
cave. The cave was only accessible at low tide, and
Tonglong had timed his arrival perfectly. In less than
an hour, his men had stripped the cave of its contents.
Now Tonglong was headed south to take care of what
he called "personal business."

ShaoShu didn't know what that business was, but
he was certain he had already gathered plenty of information for Ying and Hok. The moment he saw an
opportunity to sneak off the ship, he would make a
break for it.

Having been aboard the better part of a day and a
night, ShaoShu had learned the rhythms of the ship's
watches. The laziest sailors were assigned to the watch
that began at sunset, so that would be the best time to
make his move. In the meantime, he would just have
to wait.

From somewhere high above the deck, he heard a
lookout shout, "Sail ho!"

"What do you see?" Tonglong asked, his metallic
voice too close for ShaoShu's comfort.

"It's a foreign sloop, sir," the lookout replied. "By the shape of the stern and the rake of the mast, I'd guess she's Dutch-built. Single mast with a reefed mainsail and a storm jib set taut. She's fast, sir, and sailed by seasoned seamen. No question about it, the way that rigging is set. She's off our stern, if you'd like to have a look."

"Has anyone found my telescope yet?" Tonglong roared.

No one replied.

Tonglong stormed across the deck. "Whoever stole it will be strung up in the rigging for the birds to pluck out his eyes and feast on his liver!"

Uh-oh, ShaoShu thought, silently taking Tonglong's spyglass off his lap and placing it on the treasure pile.

"Can you see who's aboard?" Tonglong called to the lookout.

"Aye, sir. Looks to be a bunch of children, if you can believe it. Four boys and a girl. At least, I think it's a girl. She's in a dress."

ShaoShu's heart leaped. That had to be Hok, along with some helpers! Maybe Ying was with her, too. ShaoShu had last seen Hok at the apothecary shop, and she must have figured out where he'd gone. She was coming to rescue him! Hok and Ying were the smartest, kindest, bravest people he'd ever met.

"What would you like me to do, sir?" someone asked Tonglong.

"If they get close enough, blow them out of the water. People in this region need to learn to steer clear of me."

A large lump formed in ShaoShu's throat. He'd forgotten about the gigantic *qiangs,* or cannons, as the sailors called them, lashed to the deck rails.

As he tried to decide what to do next, a quick darting movement caught ShaoShu's eye. He froze, and his nose twitched. He locked his gaze on the far side of the tarp and saw a small brown blur darting about close to the ground. A mouse! He couldn't believe his good luck.

ShaoShu relaxed, grateful for the company. He reached into the folds of his dirty robe and fished out the remains of a bean-paste bun he'd swiped from a sailor earlier. ShaoShu dropped a few crumbs on the treasure pile around him and sat perfectly still. A moment later, the mouse scurried over, greedily consuming the sweet treat.

As the mouse was finishing its snack, ShaoShu gently held out a larger piece, away from his body. The small furry creature hurried over and began to nibble on ShaoShu's offering. ShaoShu smiled. He had always had good luck getting animals to come to him.

ShaoShu began to slowly, carefully, move his free hand toward the mouse to pet it when a second blur of movement, this time white, caught his eye. His body went rigid. He had had enough experience living on the streets to know what it was.

Dropping the bun, he scooped up the mouse and slipped it into one of the empty pouches he always had tied to his sash. The mouse squeaked in protest, and a white head with long flowing fur poked beneath the tarp. It was a cat.

The cat hissed, and a voice called out, "Mao? What is it? Have you found something?"

Before ShaoShu could react, the tarp was thrown back and he found himself staring into a pair of the palest brown eyes he'd ever seen. The stone-faced young man glanced at the shiny telescope on the treasure pile; then he called out to Tonglong.

"Sir, I believe I've found your thief."

CHAPTER 2

Charles stood at the helm of his sloop, breathing the clean salty air. Finally, he was in his element. No more crowded streets, no more fight clubs, and best of all, no more kung fu. They were at sea. This was the place for long-range cannon and musket fire and pistols up close. Tiger-claw fists, backflips, and flying sidekicks had no business here.

Even so, Charles glanced up at the very top of his sleek boat's single mast. Perched there was one of the best martial artists he had ever seen, a small eleven-year-old boy named Malao, or Monkey. At the base of the mast stood another kung fu master, twelve-year-old Fu, the Tiger. Fu and Malao had been sailing with him for several days, and Charles was impressed by the speed with which they had learned to help sail the boat. He supposed their lifetime of rigid training helped them learn new physical tasks quickly.

Two more young kung fu masters were also with them, though they had only come aboard a few hours earlier. The first was his good friend, a girl named Hok, or Crane, who was nearly thirteen years old. The second was a sixteen-year-old he hardly knew named Ying, or Eagle. Ying had saved Charles' life in a skirmish with Tonglong weeks ago, even getting shot in the process of distracting Tonglong so that Charles could flee. However, Charles was still finding it difficult to trust Ying. Partly because it was impossible to read Ying's facial expressions. He'd had his nose, cheeks, and forehead carved and the grooves tattooed green so that he would resemble a dragon. Charles, a Dutch, blond-haired, blue-eyed fifteen-year-old from distant Holland, would never understand these strange Chinese. Why a teenager would carve his face or why a girl would take an animal name was beyond him.

There was no denying Charles had affection for Hok, and she had asked for his help. So he was helping her. He would do almost anything for her, but what she was proposing now was out of the question.

"I am sorry," Charles said for the third time. "We have to turn around. Tonglong's crew has spotted us."

Hok stared at him, unblinking, then turned away. She adjusted a large bag of medicinal herbs over her shoulder and grabbed a spyglass from Ying.

Ying turned to Charles. "I thought you said this

boat was fast? Can't we outrun them? Let's at least get a little closer and see what we're up against before you decide to run away."

"I'll tell you what we're up against," Charles replied. "I had a clean sweep of their deck with my spyglass. They have fourteen twelve-pound cannons and at least ten soldiers with muskets. I have two pistols. We don't stand a chance. I can outrun them, sure, but we can't get any closer than this. Those big guns can nearly reach us as it is. I'm turning around."

Hok uttered a soft cry, and Charles looked over to see her gaze fixed in the direction of Tonglong's man-o-war. "Oh, no!" Hok said. "They've found him! A sailor just lifted the tarp ShaoShu was hiding under. Take a look." She held the spyglass out to Charles, but he didn't take it.

Hok's face turned bitter, and she handed the spyglass to Ying.

Charles shook his head. What didn't they understand? He was the captain of this vessel, and he had announced his decision. They were turning around.

"Crew, ready to jibe!" Charles commanded.

Fu and Malao glanced at him questioningly.

"I said, ready to jibe!" Charles repeated. "On the double!"

Fu and Malao sprang into action. Fu grabbed the jib sheet while Malao gripped a large block and tackle dangling high overhead. Hok and Ying were about to learn who was the boss.

"Jibe ho!" Charles shouted, and spun the wheel hard.

"What?" Hok and Ying asked in unison.

The boat lurched heavily to one side, and Malao shrieked, "Duck!"

Hok and Ying dropped to the deck, barely avoiding the heavy boom as it swung powerfully across the boat from port to starboard.

"Nice move, sister!" Malao said. "Me and Fu were both knocked overboard the first time Charles did that!"

Charles nodded appreciatively. He, too, was impressed by Hok's and Ying's reflexes. He continued the turn until they were pointing away from Tonglong's boat. The wind filled the sloop's sails once more, and they began racing away from the man-o-war. Charles looked back over the stern and was relieved to see that Tonglong's ship showed no signs of following or firing upon them.

Ying stood on unsteady legs and leaned his dragon face in close to Charles' face. Ying bared his sharpened teeth and flicked out his forked tongue. "Don't you *ever* do that again without telling us first," he hissed.

"Do what?" Charles asked. "Jibe?"

"Whatever it is you call turning around. That wooden pole nearly took our heads off."

"It's called a *boom*," Charles said. "And I gave you both fair warning. If you want to sail on *my* boat, you need to learn the language of the sea traders."

Ying spat over the side rail. "Sea traders? *Pirates* is more like it."

Charles felt his face begin to redden, his cheeks

hot against the cold autumn wind. With great effort, he held his tongue—and his pistols—for Hok's sake. He knew how much she disliked violence.

Hok stood and brushed off her dress. She adjusted her herb bag, then laid a hand softly on Ying's shoulder. "There is no point in arguing. That would only waste time and energy. What we need now is a plan, as our temple brother Seh would say."

"Where is that sneaky snake, anyway?" Ying asked.

"He is with friends," Hok replied. "A group of honorable bandits that includes his father. Seh has been injured."

"Oh," Ying said, not seeming to care.

Malao swung down from the masthead and joined them on deck. He poked Charles in the side. "Well, matey, where are we shoving off to now?"

"We need to discuss it," Charles said, gazing at Hok. He really did feel bad about abandoning her friend.

Hok said nothing.

"I want to help you, Hok," Charles said. "I am truly sorry about ShaoShu. However, sometimes the best course of action is retreat. That doesn't mean we can't attack later when the conditions are more favorable to us."

"What do you suggest, then?" Hok asked, not looking at him.

"I have friends in the area. We will go to them. They live on an island not far from here and—"

Ying cleared his throat and tapped Hok on the

shoulder with a long fingernail. Hok's eyes widened as something unspoken passed between them.

"What?" Charles asked.

Ying turned his back to Charles and stared out to sea.

"What is it?" Charles asked again. "I can't help you if you're keeping secrets from me."

"It's Ying's mother," Hok replied.

Charles thought for a moment, then slapped his pale forehead. "Of course! How could I have forgotten? She was injured by Tonglong and his men before they took the treasure, right?"

"That's right," Hok said.

"So you want to go back up the river, to the creek mouth bordered by twin pagodas?" Charles asked.

"Yes," Hok replied.

"Then why didn't you just say so?" Charles said. "Hang on!"

"**W**ell, well, well," Tonglong said, adjusting his ponytail braid over his shoulder and tucking the end into the sash around his waist. "What do we have here?"

ShaoShu swallowed hard, fighting the urge to glance away from Tonglong's piercing gaze. He had encountered his fair share of bullies, and he knew that you had to stand up to them. You had to stare them straight in the eye.

"My name is ShaoShu," ShaoShu replied.

"Hmm, Little Mouse?" Tonglong smirked and looked at the young man beside him at the ship's rail—the young man who had caught ShaoShu. "What do you make of the boy's name?"

"It seems fitting to me, considering the manner in which he was found," the young man replied.

The man was, of course, referring to the cat. Trying his best to look offended, ShaoShu stared at the young man. He appeared to be nearly twenty years old and looked Chinese, but he had pale brown eyes and wore his black hair close cropped. Instead of a typical Chinese robe and pants, he dressed like a Round Eye sailor—long trousers with pockets, buckled shoes, and a billowing shirt that was bound at the wrists. His white cat was at his feet, weaving its way between his ankles.

ShaoShu felt the mouse in his sash pouch begin to squirm, and he turned to Tonglong.

"ShaoShu," Tonglong said. "Is that your real name?"

"It's the only thing anyone has ever called me," ShaoShu answered.

"How old are you?"

"I don't know."

"What do you mean you don't know?"

"I don't have any parents," ShaoShu replied. "There's never been anyone to tell me how old I am or when my birthday is. I guess I'm about seven years old."

Tonglong nodded. "You're an orphan?"

"Yes."

Tonglong pointed to the young man at his side, now leaning against the ship's side rail. "He also has a unique name. He is called Lei, or Thunder. He is the chief gunner of this vessel."

Unsure of how he should reply, ShaoShu bowed.

Lei nodded.

"When was the last time you ate something, ShaoShu?" Tonglong asked.

ShaoShu suddenly grew nervous. This sounded like a trick question. He'd swiped the bean-paste bun during the night, but he didn't want to confess it. On the other hand, he didn't want to lie to a man like Tonglong. Perhaps Tonglong had even seen the remains of the bun on the treasure pile from when ShaoShu fed the mouse and already knew the answer to his own question.

ShaoShu lowered his eyes. "I stole a bean-paste bun from a soldier on deck last night, sir."

Tonglong frowned. "You stole something from one of my men? Right here on deck?"

"I am very sorry, sir," ShaoShu said, looking up. "I know I shouldn't have taken the bun, and I really shouldn't have taken your spyglass. Sometimes I just can't help myself. Please don't string me up from the rigging for the birds to eat my liver."

Tonglong rubbed his chin. "Where did you find my spyglass?"

"You left it over there last night," ShaoShu said, pointing to a small table bolted to the deck at the ship's stern.

"You didn't enter my cabin?" Tonglong asked.

ShaoShu's eyes widened. "Never, sir!"

Tonglong looked at ShaoShu suspiciously. "What are you doing on my ship?"

Despite the chilly breeze on deck, ShaoShu began to sweat. He had been practicing his response in case he got caught. "I needed to . . . I mean, I *wanted* to . . . leave the city. The city of Hangzhou."

"You're a thief, aren't you, ShaoShu?" Tonglong said.

ShaoShu didn't reply.

"What did you steal in Hangzhou?"

ShaoShu was definitely in over his head now. He hated lying, because he had a difficult time keeping his lies straight. However, there was no way he could tell Tonglong what he was really doing there.

"I stole some trinkets," ShaoShu lied.

Tonglong said nothing, obviously expecting more information.

ShaoShu sighed. Not wanting to get too deep into the lie, he decided to tell Tonglong a true story that once happened to him in the city of Xuzhou, where he used to live.

"I tried to sell the trinkets to get some money to buy food," ShaoShu said. "Except the street vendor I tried to sell them to recognized them. They belonged to someone he knew. He grabbed me, locked me in a bamboo fish trap, and went to find the judge. I escaped and wanted to run away. A boat sounded good. Yours was the first one I saw."

"A fish trap?" Tonglong said. "How did you escape from it?"

ShaoShu bit his lower lip, realizing that he should

have picked a different story. He didn't like people knowing about his secret.

"Answer my question," Tonglong said.

ShaoShu frowned. "I can squeeze through tight spaces."

"How tight?"

"Really tight."

"You're a contortionist?"

"I don't know that word. I'm just really flexible."

"Let me get this straight," Tonglong said. "You managed to stow away on *my* ship back in Hangzhou, and you avoided being detected the entire time we loaded? Then you stole my spyglass in plain sight and took a bun from a soldier on deck, all without anyone catching the slightest glimpse of you. You can also squeeze into tight spaces?"

ShaoShu nodded. "I am very sorry, sir. I understand if you want to kill me. You wouldn't be the first person to feel that way."

"Kill you?" Tonglong said with a laugh. "I'm going to hire you!" He turned to Lei. "Find an empty bunk for ShaoShu and make sure he gets a decent dinner tonight, as well as breakfast tomorrow. The two of you are to meet me on deck at sunrise. We should be in port by then. I have something special I want the two of you to help me with."

"Aye, aye, sir," Lei replied.

ShaoShu didn't like the look on Tonglong's face. He swallowed hard, and the mouse in his pouch began to squirm again.

ShaoShu cleared his throat. "Excuse me, sir, but what if I can't do the job for you? I'm just a kid, you know."

Tonglong's face grew suddenly serious, and ShaoShu felt the Mantis's black eyes drill deep into his heart.

"Then I will kill you, kid."

The sun was low in the sky by the time Charles dropped anchor in the Qiantang River. He saw no other boats nearby and no sign of Tonglong's men, but he was not about to take any chances. He was going to bring along his guns.

Charles opened his sea chest and removed a heavy sailcloth bag that had been coated with a thick layer of beeswax. He pulled his matching pistols from the folds of his Chinese-style robe, placed the pistols and his spyglass carefully into the waxed sailcloth bag, and lashed the bag closed with a length of sturdy rope.

He handed Hok a second waxed bag to protect her herb bag and tied his own bag across his back. "Let's go," Charles said.

Ying nodded and dove into the river first. Hok followed close behind, her bag slung over her shoulders. Malao let out a squeal and leaped into the water from high atop the mast, and Fu flopped over the side with a tremendous splash.

Charles scanned the shore, saw nothing, and plunged into the river. The water was cold enough to make him catch his breath. He made it to shore after a few dozen powerful strokes and, once on the bank, regretted not having packed some dry clothes in the waterproof bag. Until they had time to build a fire and dry out a bit, they would be miserable in this chilly autumn air.

Charles stopped to untie the sailcloth bag from his back and saw Ying already walking up the creek, keeping to the dense cover on one side. Ying had obviously done this type of thing before. He motioned for Charles to hurry.

Charles did not normally take direction from someone nearly his own age, but he decided to let Ying run this mission for now. After all, it was Ying's mother they were trying to save. That morning, Tonglong had triggered an avalanche inside a cave beyond his mother's house, and she was still trapped inside.

Charles removed the items from the waxed bag and retied it across his back, slipping the spyglass and one pistol into the folds of his robe. With his second pistol in hand, he silently hurried after Ying and the others. In no time, they reached a cluster of low trees near a bend in the creek, where Ying brought them to a halt. They ducked behind the foliage.

As Ying stared around the bend, Charles glanced at the towering hillsides that seemed to have sprung up from nowhere. By the river, the land was flat. Here, there was nothing but steep tree-covered slopes and rocky outcroppings. Ying moved to one side, and Charles fixed his gaze beyond him. He saw a small brick ruin that must have been Ying's mother's house.

Charles pulled the spyglass from his robe and fo-cused it on the smoldering structure. He saw tendrils of black smoke drifting from gaping holes in a green tile roof, and ornate stone dragons at each of the roof's four corners that had cracked and crumbled from intense heat. The front door was missing, and all the wooden window lattices and shutters had been burned away.

"There's been a fire," Charles said, lowering the spyglass.

"I see that," Ying replied. "What do you think, Pussy-cat? Is it empty?"

Fu's eyes narrowed, and he turned one ear in the direction of the house. After a moment, he said, "I don't see or hear anything."

Ying nodded. "I thought I sensed something, but maybe it's just my anger giving me confused signals. The house was not like this when I left. Someone has burned it since." He spat.

"What should we do?" Malao asked in a nervous tone. "Maybe it was soldiers."

"It probably was," Ying replied. "I doubt anyone is here now, though. I don't think this is a trap. If it was, they wouldn't have burned everything. They would have left the house intact to draw me in. I'm going in, regardless. We're going to need light to see inside the cave, and I'm going to try making some torches. You can all wait here."

Ying stood suddenly and strode out into the open, heading straight for the house at a brisk pace.

"Wait!" Hok called, but Ying didn't stop.

Charles, Hok, Fu, and Malao all scanned the surrounding hillsides, looking for trouble. Ying passed into the house without incident.

"I don't see anything strange," Hok said.

"Me either," Fu said. "But it feels wrong to me. Let's hurry up and help Lizard Boy. The sooner we get out of here, the better."

"Yeah, let's hurry," Malao added.

Hok nodded and stood, stepping out into the open. Fu and Malao stepped after her.

"You three go on ahead," Charles said, scanning the area with his spyglass. "I'll keep a lookout until you're inside the house."

"Good idea," Hok said. She and the others jogged over to the house. Once they were inside, Charles lowered the spyglass, sat back, and scratched his head. Like Fu, he had an uneasy feeling.

If I was going to set a trap for Ying, Charles thought, *how would I do it?*

He decided that he probably *would* burn the

house. If the house was left untouched, Ying might have little reason to ever enter it again. However, if it had been torched, he would likely enter it to inspect the damage.

Charles also concluded that he would not bother to set up an ambush inside the house. Instead, he would post a sniper in a well-concealed location outside, preferably high up. Every ship he had ever sailed in had snipers aboard, men who would climb high aloft in the rigging and rain musket balls down upon enemy ships. A person high overhead armed with a musket could cover a surprising amount of ground.

Raising the spyglass to his eye once more, he looked both high and low this time. It took nearly a quarter of an hour, but he finally found him. Perched in a tree directly opposite the rear of the house sat a man in a silky red and green robe and pants that blended almost perfectly with the autumn foliage. The sniper had one musket raised to his shoulder, trained upon the house, and several more in a large sling next to him. Charles realized that the house must have a back door, and if anyone stepped through it, they would be dead.

Charles needed to act. He raised his pistol to better gauge the distance between himself and the sniper, but it was just as he'd suspected. He was too far away to have any hope of his lead ball reaching its target.

As Charles contemplated what to do next, Malao wandered out the front door, staring at his toes. He stopped and lifted one foot all the way up to his nose, wiggling his toes and giggling loudly as the others began to scold him from within the house. They told him to stay out there because his feet stank so much. How his feet could still smell so bad even after swimming in the river, they would never know.

Charles looked back at the sniper and saw with horror that he was repositioning his musket. It seemed he had a clear shot at anyone coming out the front door, too.

Charles leaped from the undergrowth and rushed toward Malao, yelling at the top of his lungs, "Ahoy! Malao! Sniper in a tree! JUMP, MATEY!"

Malao sprang high into the air. At the same moment, a cloud of dust mushroomed beneath his feet, followed by a loud *CRACK!* that pierced the chilly air.

"We're under fire!" Charles shouted. "Take cover!"

As he headed for the front door, hoping to reach it before the sniper took up another musket, Charles watched to see where Malao landed. However, Malao never hit the ground. Charles looked up, astonished, and saw Malao scrambling about the rooftop.

"Hot, hot, hot!" Malao screeched.

Roof tiles exploded next to Malao, followed by the crisp report of the sniper's second musket. Those lead balls were fast. They were making impact before their blast could be heard. The man in the tree had top-notch equipment and fresh powder.

Charles watched Malao drop into the house through one of the large holes in the roof. Charles looked back at the sniper and saw that the man had taken up a third musket. This one was aimed directly at Charles.

Charles raised his pistol and cocked back the flint-tipped hammer, assuming the worst. The sniper was stationary with a long-barreled musket that was guaranteed to be far more accurate than Charles' short pistol. What was worse, Charles was barely within range for his weapon. By all accounts, he didn't stand a chance.

A tremendous growl suddenly filled the air, and with his eyes still fixed on the sniper, Charles saw a large piece of stone sailing toward the tree. The sniper saw it, too, and the instant the man's head shifted slightly in the direction of the flying object, Charles fired his pistol.

Bang!

Thud.

The sniper hit the ground in a heap.

Charles raced toward the man, but Fu got there first and gave the sniper a swift kick to the kidneys. Charles was not surprised when the man didn't budge.

Fu rolled the man over, and they saw that the lead ball had passed deep into the center of his chest. A fallen piece of one of the stone dragons was lodged in the sniper's forehead, the skin around it blistering curiously.

Fu growled, softer this time, and Charles saw that he was holding his right hand. Fu's palm was swelling fast. Charles realized that the stone shard Fu had thrown was burning hot.

"I can't believe you threw hot stone," Charles said as the others hurried over. "Thank you, Fu. Nice throw."

Fu shrugged.

Hok took Fu's injured hand in her own, inspecting

it. "You'll be fine," she said. "Go dip it into the cool water of the creek. I'll make a salve and wrap your hand as we walk to Ying's mother."

Fu grunted and headed for the creek.

Hok shifted the waxed sailcloth bag containing her herbs and turned to Charles. "Are you okay?"

"I'm all right," Charles replied, "but I'm worried about Fu. Malao, too. He was jumping around barefoot on those hot roof tiles."

Malao hobbled over, grinning. "You're worried about me? Don't bother." He lifted a small dirty foot and wiggled his toes. Other than black ash on his sole and a few blades of burnt grass wedged beneath his toenails, Malao's foot looked fine, though its smell left something to be desired.

"It would take a lot more than a little heat to get through my thick soles," Malao said. "Besides, I've danced across hot roof tiles before." He giggled. "The same thing goes for Fu's hand. All his years of Iron Palm and Tiger Claw training have thickened his skin and killed most of his nerve endings. I bet he didn't feel a thing."

Charles shook his head. He never would understand these foreigners.

"Thanks for saving me, by the way, Charles," Malao said.

"No, no," Charles replied. "We should all thank Fu. If he hadn't—"

Ying stepped up to the group. "You can congratulate each other later. Right now, we need to keep moving." He glanced down at the sniper and paused, bending over. He seized the sniper's left forearm and said, "Did you notice this?"

Charles looked down and saw that the man had a jellyfish tattooed on the inside of his left wrist. "Does it mean something?" he asked.

"This region is controlled by the Southern Warlord, a man called HaiZhe, or Jellyfish. I was introduced to him at a fight club once. This man works for him."

"What is he doing here?" Hok asked.

"I have no idea," Ying said. "We'll have to figure it out later."

Ying led them back to the ruined house, where he had assembled several torches. They were fashioned out of furniture legs wrapped with cloth and soaked in some kind of liquid. Beside the torches was a small container that held a glowing ember.

"There is one bedroom that didn't burn," Ying said in response to Charles' questioning glances. "In it we found a pot of lamp oil, plus some bedsheets and a few wooden chairs. That's how I made these." He picked up the torches. "I want to save them for inside the cave, so let's try to reach it while there's still daylight."

After nearly an hour of climbing in the waning daylight, they reached the small back entrance to the cave where Ying's mother lay. Charles volunteered to guard the entry with three muskets that they'd taken from the fallen sniper, while the others lit the torches and rushed into the cave, armed with thick tree branches to use as levers.

Charles sat down with a heavy sigh and glanced about in the dim light. The coast appeared to be clear. With one corner of his robe, he began to clean his pistol as best he could and felt like kicking himself for not having brought additional shot, powder, and wads for reloading.

He had hardly finished wiping down his pistol when the others came plodding out of the cave. They were dusty and sullen, and Ying's mother lay limp and motionless in Ying's arms. Charles saw streaks running down Ying's cheeks where tears had wiped strips of his dirty face clean.

Charles knew better than to ask questions. They had arrived too late. Bitterly disappointed, he grabbed his pistol and the muskets and followed the others silently down the steep hillside. It took them longer to get back to the house in the dark. Fu went in ahead of them to investigate with his extraordinary low-light vision and declared that all was secure.

Once inside the house, Charles stood with his back against one of the brick walls, which was still warm from the house's demise. It provided some relief from the ever-increasing chill of the night. His clothes, like everyone else's, were still damp. Fu and Malao set about gathering kindling for a fire, while Ying took his mother into the undamaged bedroom. Hok walked over to Charles and began to rummage through her herb bag. Where they stood, a sliver of starlight shone through one of the gaping holes in the roof, providing at least some light.

"This is really sad," Charles said.

Hok nodded but didn't reply.

"What was Ying's mother's name?"

"WanSow," Hok said. "It means 'Cloud Hand.' Ying said that she was a *Tai Chi* master."

"What is *Tai Chi*?" Charles asked.

"It is a Chinese martial art that combines moving meditation with specialized breathing techniques."

"What is so special about breathing?"

Hok stopped rummaging and pulled out a section of evergreen branch. She looked deeply into Charles' eyes. "If you stop breathing, you stop living."

Charles didn't know how to respond to that.

Hok continued. "But imagine if you could control your breathing to the point where you almost stop but don't."

"I don't understand," Charles said. "Is there a difference between almost stopping and actually stopping? I mean, how do you *almost* stop breathing?"

"For most people like you and me," Hok said, "no, there is no difference. For WanSow, however, there may be. Come watch."

Hok led Charles to a small room, where they found Ying kneeling beside his mother. Fu and Malao had started a fire nearby, and they were already beginning to warm themselves near it. Hok kneeled next to Ying, beside WanSow.

"This is a branch from the *xiang mu* tree," Hok said, showing it to Ying in the flickering firelight. "No living person can inhale the odor of its sap without stirring."

"Let me do it," Ying said.

Charles watched as Hok handed the small branch to Ying. Ying bent it several times, back and forth, then twisted it around and around upon itself. Charles could just make out a tiny bubble of liquid that had risen where Ying had bent and twisted the branch. Ying waved the bubble slowly beneath his mother's nose, and to Charles' surprise, she stirred.

Ying pulled the branch away, and WanSow weakly opened her eyes. She blinked twice at Ying, slowly, and Charles thought that he saw the slightest hint of a smile on her face before her eyelids drifted closed once more.

"I don't believe it," Charles said. "Ying, I give you joy!"

Ying nodded. "Thank you," he said.

Malao squealed with delight. "Is she going to be okay?"

"We'll have to wait and see," Hok said. "It could be days before we know for sure. Maybe weeks."

Charles' blond eyebrows shot up his freckled forehead. "Weeks? Can we move her before then?"

"It depends," Hok said. "We shouldn't move her until we know the extent of her internal damage. There is no telling how long that will be."

"But we can't stay here," Charles said, looking up at the holes in the roof.

"Sure we can," Malao replied. "Fu and I once helped rebuild an entire village after Tonglong and his men burned it. We can fix this place up in no time."

"What about the sniper?" Charles said. "Won't somebody miss him?"

"That is a concern, to be sure," Hok said. "But I'm even more concerned about WanSow."

"I'll take care of any more snipers," Fu growled.

Ying stood. "We all appreciate your concern, Charles. However, you are highly skilled with your pistols, and I've handled my fair share of muskets. Thanks to the sniper, we have three, fully loaded. Besides, I know something of the posting of snipers, and they nearly always work individually and on one-week rotations. Sometimes they'll stay posted for an entire month. Chances are very good that no one will miss him for a while."

"I can't leave my sloop out there for an entire month," Charles said. "Or even a week. Someone will steal it. Just leaving it empty overnight makes me nervous."

"Then go to it," Hok said. "Pull up your anchor, too, if you wish. However, please don't go far. I know a safe place we can take WanSow once she's stabilized, but we will need your help to get her there."

Charles frowned. What he wanted to do was take them to visit his sailor friends on the nearby island. Ever since they'd turned away from Tonglong's ship, he'd been thinking about meeting up with his mates. He longed for a good old-fashioned Dutch meal and the chance to speak his native tongue again. What's more, there was a good chance they would meet up with someone Hok would certainly want to see as much as he did—her father, Captain Henrik. Hok hadn't seen him since she was very young, but the last Charles had heard, Captain Henrik was on his way to the island. However, Charles dared not mention the possibility of her seeing her father for fear of giving her false hope. Captain Henrik was always on the move.

Frustrated and confused, Charles headed for the burned-out doorway. "When you are ready, meet me at the creek mouth. I will be aboard my sloop, waiting."

€arly the next morning, ShaoShu stood on the deck of Tonglong's warship, watching the sun begin to rise through thick morning fog. Lei stood next to him, dressed in a fine Chinese military uniform instead of the previous day's foreign sailor's outfit. As his cat prowled the deck a few paces away, Lei plucked white cat hairs from his red silk robe and pants. ShaoShu felt the mouse in his pouch grow restless.

"Ready, Lei?" asked a metallic voice behind ShaoShu. He turned to see Tonglong dressed in an immaculate silk uniform identical to Lei's, a shining straight sword tucked into his brilliant white sash.

"I am ready for anything, sir," Lei replied.

"Anything?" Tonglong asked, adjusting his long ponytail braid over his shoulder. "Prove it."

In a flash, Lei whipped off his sash, and his red robe fell open to reveal two thick straps of leather crisscrossing his chest. Each strap held three small loaded pistols in holsters and several small pouches. Before ShaoShu could even blink, Lei had a pistol in each hand.

"Excellent," Tonglong said. "I've heard good things about you."

Lei bowed.

Tonglong turned to ShaoShu. "Lei is coming along to provide protection. You will accompany me as my servant. I don't expect any trouble, but it's better to be safe than sorry. Lei has a reputation for being a first-rate gunner with ships' cannons, but he is perhaps even better known for his pistols. Have you ever heard of the fight clubs, ShaoShu?"

ShaoShu's eyes widened. He had indeed heard of the fight clubs. He looked at Lei, amazed. "You're *that* Thunder?"

"At your service," Lei replied, retying his sash.

"You're famous!" ShaoShu said. "They say the Grand Championship will probably be between you and the fighter known as Golden Dragon."

"That is probably true," Lei said, his eyes twinkling. "And I have no doubt that I will be victorious." He patted the pistols beneath his robe. "It will be the highest honor for me to win the Grand Championship and join the ranks of such men as General Tonglong."

And Ying, ShaoShu thought, hiding a smile. He

couldn't help feeling excited. Everybody knew about the fight clubs. Even though he had never been inside one, being a friend to Ying—last year's Grand Champion—made him feel proud.

Tonglong looked at Lei. "I have never seen you in action, but my mother has. While some people question the use of pistols in the pit arena, she applauds it. I am not sure how I feel about it."

"The rules say that any weapon may be used, sir," Lei said. "The pistol just happens to be the ultimate weapon. There is nothing preventing other participants from using pistols, but most don't because firearms have drawbacks. Many times they don't fire, and when they do, you get only one shot. Also, if you mishandle it, you might shoot a spectator. I believe that disqualifies you."

"So it does," Tonglong said. "It would indeed be a shame to be disqualified because of a spectator. My mother believes that you have the skills required to win this year's title. She is the one who suggested I have you join my ship's crew, you know."

"I did not know that, sir. I had the honor of meeting her earlier this year. She is very knowledgeable about the fight clubs, and she said that your father was once an acquaintance of my father. I remember AnGangseh well."

The corners of Tonglong's thin lips rose up into a devious grin. "She is not easy to forget."

"Might she be in Shanghai, sir? The fight club finale is to be held there in two months, and with your permission I hope to be given leave to participate. If she is there, I would enjoy seeing her again."

"She will be there," Tonglong said. "She is currently en route, entertaining the Emperor. I will be there, too, as will many of the former Grand Champions. Of course you will be given leave. I know more than anyone the extent to which winning can change your life. I shall reintroduce you to my mother, too. I may even introduce you to the Emperor."

Lei looked away. "That would be most kind of you, sir."

Tonglong nodded and turned to ShaoShu. "Perhaps I will bring you as well. Would you like that?"

ShaoShu's eyes lit up. "Yes, sir!"

"Good," Tonglong said. "Prove yourself today, and I will bring you along. Come, let us see what you are made of."

Tonglong led ShaoShu and Lei down the ship's gangway to an enormous dock. The morning fog was beginning to burn off, and ShaoShu now had a better view of the wharf. It wasn't at all what he'd expected.

There were perhaps a hundred docks along the shoreline, but only a handful of boats were tied up there. Of those, every one was battered and ancient and very small, just big enough to hold two or three fishermen. None of them looked like the elaborate trading vessels ShaoShu was used to seeing in other ports.

Beyond the docks stood more than thirty buildings, but most of them had fallen in upon themselves, and only one appeared to be occupied. This was nothing at all like Hangzhou or any of the other waterside cities ShaoShu had seen before. This was a ghost town.

Tonglong stepped off the docks and walked briskly up the wharf, and ShaoShu hurried to keep pace. Lei stayed well behind, his head constantly rotating from side to side as he looked for trouble.

They approached the only building with an OPEN sign, and before they could knock, an elderly woman came out to greet them. She said that she hadn't had a customer in weeks and begged them to join her for tea. Tonglong declined, saying that they were in a hurry and simply needed to purchase a few things. He handed her a list, and she disappeared inside.

The woman returned holding a large sack, and Tonglong nodded to ShaoShu. She handed the sack to him to carry.

"*Ooof,*" ShaoShu said, struggling beneath its bulk. "What's in here?"

"You'll find out soon enough," Tonglong said. "Lei, pay the woman."

Tonglong led ShaoShu away. They had taken only a few steps when ShaoShu began to lose his grip on the unwieldy sack. It wasn't so much that it was heavy; it was nearly half as tall as he was, and he couldn't see a thing while he carried it. It flopped around in front of him, blocking his view. All he could do was follow behind Tonglong, keeping his eyes glued to Tonglong's feet, trying his best not to trip over the

uneven pavement stones as they wound their way in-
land up a dilapidated road.

Half an hour later, ShaoShu was in agony. His
arms and legs were beginning to shake from holding the sack in awkward positions, and his back felt
like it was going to snap in two. In an effort to
distract his mind from the discomfort, he said to
Tonglong, "Excuse me, sir, may I ask where we are
going?"

"Where do you think we are going?" Tonglong
replied.

"This sack smells like it has food in it. Are we going to visit someone?"

"We are, indeed," Tonglong said.

"Are we going to a party?" ShaoShu asked, growing excited. "I love parties!"

"You could call it a party."

"Who is the party for?"

"My father."

ShaoShu frowned. *Didn't Tonglong just say that his
mother was with the Emperor?* he thought.

"Is there something you wish to ask?" Tonglong
said.

ShaoShu swallowed hard. "I was just thinking about
your mother."

"Ah, yes. AnGangseh—the Cobra. Even if she were
in this village, she would not accompany us. She has
moved on from my father. Indeed, she has moved on
from her second husband, too. She is not the most
loyal person."

"Oh," replied ShaoShu.

"Any more questions before we arrive?"

ShaoShu scratched his head. "Do you have any brothers or sisters, sir?"

"I have a half brother from my mother's second marriage. He is called Seh, or Snake. He is a young warrior monk."

ShaoShu nearly choked. Seh was Hok's temple brother! Afraid to ask any more questions, ShaoShu trudged on until Tonglong stopped suddenly.

ShaoShu crashed into the back of Tonglong's legs, and Tonglong's knees buckled slightly, but he didn't seem to notice. His eyes were fixed straight ahead, and he appeared to be lost in thought.

"We have arrived," Tonglong said drily. "Let the party begin."

ShaoShu gratefully set the sack down. He peeked around Tonglong to see where the party would take place, and his mouth dropped open. They were standing at the gates of a cemetery.

"What's wrong?" Tonglong asked. "You're not superstitious, are you?"

"No," ShaoShu replied, lying.

Tonglong smirked. "You have nothing to fear from spirits. Unless you've angered them, of course. Have you ever been to a cemetery?"

ShaoShu shook his head.

"This cemetery has degraded miserably since my father's death, as has the entire village. This was home, and he built it into a prosperous port. Without his leadership, it has fallen into ruin. I haven't been here in many years. I hope my father isn't upset with me."

ShaoShu shivered. So did his mouse.

Tonglong walked through the gates, and ShaoShu reluctantly picked up the sack and headed in after him. He looked back over his shoulder and saw Lei stop near the entrance, where he pulled a pistol from the folds of his robe and stood guard. ShaoShu almost laughed. What good would a pistol be against angry spirits?

Not wanting to upset any ghosts that might be lurking about, even in the daylight, ShaoShu continued on as silently as possible, using every trick he knew to keep his footfalls quiet. He figured that was the respectful thing to do. Tonglong, on the other hand, plodded forward, his heavy boots echoing over ancient stone paths, kicking up dust clouds in the morning sun.

They passed through several elaborate courtyards, and Tonglong led ShaoShu through a series of low buildings that had no roofs. Along every wall were neat rows of square stone plaques about the size of his head. The plaques were covered in Chinese characters, and beneath each was a narrow shelf. On a few of the shelves sat tiny vases containing dried flowers. ShaoShu wondered when they would come across gravestones, like he'd seen in other places, but there wasn't a single one in sight.

Soon they stopped in front of a small ornate building about seven paces long by five paces wide.

This one did have a roof but no doors or windows. Intricate statues as large as a man had been hewn from the black stone walls, seemingly bursting forth from the living rock. There were three, all disturbing variations of the same horrible creature—a mantis.

ShaoShu swallowed hard.

"Impressive, isn't it?" Tonglong said.

ShaoShu nodded.

"The mantis has been my family's symbol for many generations. It is fast, intelligent, and more than anything, efficient. Just like my father. Just like *me.*"

A chill ran down ShaoShu's spine. He felt like someone—or something—was watching him. He stared at the building, and high on one wall, he noticed a circular recess that contained a painting of a particularly vicious mantis. It was tearing a small bird to pieces.

ShaoShu looked away and said, "Your father is buried in there?"

"Buried? No. No one is buried in this cemetery. That is not our custom in this region. We cremate our dead, burn them to ash. The remains are collected in an urn and entombed."

ShaoShu pointed to the roofless buildings behind them. "Is that what those squares are for?"

"Yes. Behind each plaque is a small space that contains an urn. The shelves are for placing offerings. Those buildings contain generation upon generation of hundreds of families."

"But your father has a whole building to himself?"

"That's right."

"He must have been very important."

"He was, indeed."

ShaoShu looked at the ornate black building again. "How come he doesn't have a shelf?"

Tonglong chuckled. "We place his offerings on the ground, facing the painting of the mantis with the bird. Open the sack, and you can help me."

ShaoShu cringed but did as he was told. He untied the sack, and a foodlike scent that he couldn't identify wafted forth.

"What is that smell?" he asked.

"Smoked beef tongue. It was my father's favorite."

ShaoShu made a sour face.

"Don't worry," Tonglong said. "You won't be eating it. It is intended for my father's spirit only, like everything else in there."

ShaoShu began removing the rest of the bag's contents, growing more confused with each item. Besides the smoked beef tongue, he pulled out a small cask of wine, three dinner buns, three apples, three robes made of thin colorful paper, and several blocks of thick paper folded and painted to resemble bars of gold and silver.

Tonglong arranged the food and wine on the ground, then picked up the paper items and the empty sack. He led ShaoShu to a nearby fire pit that had a small lantern burning next to it, even though it was broad daylight. Tonglong put the items down and neatly unfolded one of the paper robes, laying it on the fire pit's cold ashes.

"They say even spirits need new clothes and money," Tonglong said. "People burn these likenesses to satisfy those needs. It is a way of showing that you have respect for your ancestors, respect for your past."

Tonglong picked up the lantern and opened it, lowering it to one corner of the paper robe. The robe burst into flames. As he began to unfold a second robe, he looked at ShaoShu and nodded toward a sunny courtyard. "Why don't you wait for me over there? I am going to meditate now."

"Yes, sir," ShaoShu said, glad to be getting away from the smoke and the eerie black building. He strolled over to the courtyard and sat down on a stone bench in the warm sun.

He thought about letting his mouse out to get some fresh air and sunshine, but he was concerned that it might run off. Chasing a mouse across a cemetery did not sound like fun. Besides, Tonglong would probably be finished at any moment. After all, how long could a person meditate?

Several hours later, ShaoShu was still wondering. Lunchtime had come and gone, and Tonglong hadn't budged. He sat in the same position hour after hour, unmoving, his legs crossed, his eyes closed, and his back perfectly straight. ShaoShu had never seen someone with so much discipline.

ShaoShu's stomach growled, and he glanced over at the food offerings. Even smoked beef tongue was beginning to sound better than no lunch at all. However, he saw that the food was covered with a blanket of swarming flies, and he quickly lost his appetite.

With nothing to do, ShaoShu decided to take a nap. He hadn't slept much over the past few days, and this seemed like a perfect opportunity. He closed his eyes, and after what felt like half an hour, he was startled awake by the sound of heavy boots crossing the courtyard. He wiped the sleep from his eyes and was shocked to see that it had grown dark. The moon was even beginning to rise.

"Time to get to work," Tonglong said, stopping next to ShaoShu.

"Uh, okay," ShaoShu replied, pushing himself to his feet. He made a move toward the fire pit, but Tonglong grabbed his arm.

"Where do you think you are going?"

"To get the sack."

"Why?"

"To collect the food offerings."

"No," Tonglong said. "They are to stay here."

ShaoShu looked at him, unsure what Tonglong wanted him to do.

"I didn't bring you along just to be my servant," Tonglong said.

ShaoShu glanced around at what little he could see of the cemetery, and his nose twitched. He didn't like the sound of this at all.

"What do you want me to do?"

"I need you to retrieve something."

"From where?"

Tonglong pointed to the circular painting high up the wall of his father's final resting place. The painting of the mantis tearing the bird to pieces.

"In there."

CHAPTER
6

ShaoShu glanced up at the circular mantis painting on Tonglong's father's final resting place, then at the formidable statues. There was only one thing inside that building, and ShaoShu had no interest in retrieving it.

"How do you expect me to get in there?" ShaoShu asked.

"That painting is only rice paper glued to a round wooden frame," Tonglong said. "It's called a spirit window. You can easily tear through it."

ShaoShu glanced up at the night sky and muttered, "Why did he have to wait for night?"

"I heard that," Tonglong said. "Not that it's any of your business, but I'd rather not have anyone see what you are about to do."

"I won't be able to see, either, sir!" ShaoShu protested. "I can't do it. I don't think I can squeeze through there."

"You will do it," Tonglong said. "Or you will die. Do you understand?" He gripped the straight sword sheathed neatly in his sash.

ShaoShu lowered his head, defeated. "I understand. I'm going to need a boost, though, sir."

Tonglong led ShaoShu over to the front of the small building, stepping around the food offerings. He grabbed ShaoShu by the waist and lifted him up, but ShaoShu's head was barely in line with the painting.

"I need to be higher, sir," ShaoShu said. "Can I stand on your shoulders?"

"Grab hold of the window recess."

ShaoShu gripped the lip of the recessed circle containing the mantis painting, and Tonglong let go of his waist. As he dangled there, Tonglong squatted down, grabbed ShaoShu's ankles, and planted ShaoShu's feet firmly on his shoulders before standing up again.

ShaoShu found that the bottom of the round window was now in line with his belly button. This was better. He poked at the rice paper covering the circular recess, and his fingers easily broke through.

"Tear the whole thing out and put your head in," Tonglong said. "Tell me what you see."

ShaoShu gladly tore the scary painting to pieces and threw them to the ground. He pushed against the wooden frame, and it crumbled in his hands. With the circular opening cleared, he pressed his head through it, but the rest of his body was stopped short by his shoulders. He pulled his head back out and looked down at Tonglong.

"I can't see anything, and I can't fit. Please let me down."

"No," Tonglong said. "You're not finished yet. Take hold of the recess again, and keep your balance. I'm going to squat once more." Tonglong squatted and reached down as ShaoShu teetered on Tonglong's shoulders. ShaoShu couldn't see what he was doing.

Tonglong stood, and ShaoShu maintained his grip on the window opening for support. Tonglong said, "Lower your right hand."

ShaoShu dropped his hand, and Tonglong slapped something cold and slimy into it.

"*Ew!*" ShaoShu cried. "What is it?"

"Beef tongue. Nice and slippery, thanks to the flies. Pull off your robe and wipe it against your shoulders. You'll squeeze right through."

ShaoShu paused.

"I could always cut off one of your arms instead to help you fit," Tonglong said.

Remembering Tonglong's straight sword, ShaoShu began to worry. "Why do you think I can make it, sir?"

"Because a mouse can fit its entire body inside any opening that can accommodate its head. It does so by dislocating its joints. I felt your arm earlier, and you have very loose joints, like your namesake. I suspect that you can dislocate one or even both of your shoulders without too much trouble. I can help you, if you like."

ShaoShu swallowed hard. "No, thank you, sir. I'll manage." While it was painful, he'd done it before.

He pushed his robe off his shoulders, down to his waist, and gooseflesh formed across his back and arms in the cold night air. He quickly slathered the rotting beef tongue up one shoulder and down the other, then threw it aside.

ShaoShu shoved his head back through the opening and craned his neck in the darkness of the interior. He could see nothing. He slipped his right arm and part of his right shoulder into the window and groaned. "A little higher, please, sir."

He felt Tonglong grasp his ankles, and slowly he began to rise. The moment his hips were in line with the opening, ShaoShu wrenched his right shoulder violently in toward the center of his chest. With a muffled cry and a loud *crack, squish!* he thrust his upper body through, his left arm and shoulder following with the help of the slick beef tongue juice.

He was in up to his waist.

ShaoShu took a deep breath, sweating profusely, trying to block out the tremendous pain in his dislocated right shoulder. Before he could make his next move, he felt Tonglong preparing to give him one final shove.

"No!" ShaoShu squeaked. "Not yet, sir!"

But it was too late. ShaoShu felt Tonglong twist him through the opening like a screw. An instant later, he landed in a heap on the cold stone floor, not having had a chance to pop his shoulder back into its socket. Without two arms to cushion his fall, his head struck the floor violently.

ShaoShu slipped into unconsciousness.

CHAPTER
7

53

Charles sat on the deck of his sloop, straining his eyes in the dim light of a paraffin lamp. In one hand, he held a block of flint; in the other, a large stone hammer. Raising the hammer high, Charles brought it down with great precision against a subtle crack in the flint's side. A flake roughly the size of his thumbnail sheared off, landing at his feet in a shower of sparks.

Charles smiled. He loved knapping flints in the dark. If he had enough time, he would make a whole pile of flints for his Dutch mates to use in their pistols. That would be an appropriate gift in exchange for the hospitality he would surely receive.

With thoughts of Dutch delicacies racing through his mind, and his eyes on his work, Charles didn't see the others until they were standing on the bank not fifteen swimming strokes from his sloop.

"Ahoy, matey!" Malao said. "Permission to come aboard?"

Charles set down his tools and stared at them across the short span of water. *What are they doing here already?* he wondered. It had only been one day.

"Well?" Fu growled.

"Of course you can come aboard," Charles said. "But what about Ying's mother?"

Someone coughed—a deep, wet cough—and a slender, attractive woman with long black wispy hair stepped forward from behind Ying. She bowed.

Charles was dumbstruck. It was WanSow, Ying's mother.

WanSow stumbled, and Ying grabbed her by the waist.

"Don't let her fool you, Charles," Hok said gently. "She is not as strong as she might look. She needs treatment."

"I am fine," WanSow retorted, and Charles heard a slight gurgle in her voice.

"She has fluid in her lungs," Hok explained. "Can you take us to the large apothecary in Hangzhou?"

"That is where you had planned to take her all along, isn't it?" Charles asked.

Hok nodded in the darkness. "Yes, I'd like to wait for her to get stronger, but we have to leave this location. WanSow believes others may come now that Tonglong has the treasure."

"I don't understand," Charles said.

"Tonglong stole a famous treasure hoard," Ying replied. "It included a set of legendary white jade swords and a suit of white jade armor. The swords and armor are purely symbolic, but the treasure can be used to bribe any number of officials. Remember the Southern Warlord I told you about?"

"HaiZhe?" Charles said. "Yes. I remember that sniper's tattoo."

"That's right," Ying said. "My mother has told us that HaiZhe has been after that treasure and those powerful symbols for years, and he suspects that my mother knows where the treasure was hidden. I am certain no one was spying on us before Tonglong attacked, so the sniper must have arrived afterward. HaiZhe probably sent someone to follow Tonglong's ship, and once word got back that Tonglong came here, HaiZhe posted the sniper. As soon as Tonglong starts spreading the treasure around, or HaiZhe realizes that his sniper hasn't reported back, HaiZhe will come looking for my mother. We need to leave."

"Aye, aye," Charles said. He grabbed a stout rope and tied one end to the sloop's sturdy mast. Then he hurled the remaining rope to shore and grabbed a length of sailcloth. "Pull that rope taut and tie it to a tree. I'm going to rig up a sling to get WanSow aboard. With any luck, we'll make it to the apothecary before sunrise."

CHAPTER 8

ShaoShu opened his eyes to find that he had a splitting headache, a dislocated shoulder, and no idea what time it was. Even so, he grinned as his eyes adjusted to the near pitch-black darkness. His mouse was snuggled up against his neck, nibbling on his hair. It didn't appear to have been injured while ShaoShu squeezed through the hole in the wall or when he fell.

His happiness didn't last long, however.

"ShaoShu," Tonglong called from outside the small building. "Can you hear me?"

"Umm . . . yes, sir," ShaoShu groaned, his cloudy head beginning to clear.

"Is anything broken?"

ShaoShu thought for a moment as he struggled to

pull his robe back on. "My shoulder is still out of joint and it really hurts, but I think that's all that's wrong."

"That's not what I meant," Tonglong hissed. "Did you break anything that belonged to my father?"

"I don't think so."

"Good. Look up. I have something for you."

ShaoShu looked up at the small round window and saw something float down. It was a silk bag.

"Pick it up," Tonglong said.

"Ouch," ShaoShu said with a grunt, struggling to stand with his one good arm. "I need to do something first, sir." He made it to his feet and walked to one of the walls. ShaoShu tapped it with his foot to gauge his distance in the dark.

"ShaoShu, I need you to—"

"Wait, sir, please!" ShaoShu snapped. Building up his courage, he lunged forward, slamming his right shoulder into the stone wall. *"Arrrrgh!"* he groaned between gritted teeth. He hadn't hit it quite hard enough.

"Are you—" Tonglong began.

"Please, wait!" ShaoShu squeaked. He took a step backward, then lunged forward again, ramming his shoulder into the wall a second time. *"Owwww!"* he howled, and dropped to the floor, sweating despite the chilly night air. His second attempt had been successful.

After a few deep breaths, ShaoShu stood on wobbly legs. He rotated his right shoulder and shrugged it several times. It hurt tremendously but seemed to work more or less normally. He picked up the silk bag.

"Sorry I was rude, sir," ShaoShu said in a shaky voice. "What should I do now?"

Tonglong scoffed. "The building has only one room, and you are in it. There is a heavy stone pedestal in the very center. On it rests a porcelain urn. Carefully pour the contents of the urn into the bag and throw the bag out to me."

"But, sir—" ShaoShu began to say, thinking about the contents.

"Do it."

ShaoShu bit his lip. He had no choice. Without Tonglong's assistance, he would never get out of there.

He stumbled through the darkness on his still-wobbly legs until he kicked what could only be the pedestal. He reached up for the urn and heard a sickening scrape as he accidentally bumped the fragile container with his elbow. There was a tremendous crash, and the urn shattered on the stone floor.

"ShaoShu!" Tonglong roared in his metallic voice.

"Just a moment, sir," ShaoShu said nervously. He dropped to his knees and began to hurriedly sweep the urn's contents into the bag. Soft powdery ash stuck between his sweaty fingers.

ShaoShu frowned. "I'm sorry," he whispered to Tonglong's father's spirit.

As he was finishing, ShaoShu's hand knocked against something that felt like metal. He heard a soft *clank!* as the object slid across the stone floor, striking the base of the pedestal. He slid his hand over the area until his fingers wrapped around what felt like a small key with lumps on it.

"I heard that noise," Tonglong said. "Did you find something among the ashes?"

"Yes," ShaoShu replied. "A key, I think."

"Good. Throw it to me."

ShaoShu tossed the key out the window. He heard Tonglong's hands clap together as he caught it.

The next thing ShaoShu heard was Tonglong walking away.

"Hey!" ShaoShu shouted. "Where are you going?!"

"I have what I need," Tonglong replied. "I am returning to the ship. I have much work to do."

"What about me?"

"You have served your purpose," Tonglong said, and he laughed. "I'll be sure to mention you when I rewrite history."

ShaoShu's eyes darted around the room, searching for something that might make Tonglong turn around. He remembered the silk bag.

"What about your father?" ShaoShu said in a desperate tone. "What about your past?"

"I have even less use for him now than I do for you," Tonglong replied, his voice already far away. "Goodbye, Little Mouse."

CHAPTER 9

ShaoShu felt like crying. He looked up through the blackness at the small round hole that served as a dead man's window. This was going to be *his* final resting place, too. His body would rot beside Tonglong's father's ashes.

He sniffled. There was no way he could reach the window. Even if he could climb onto the pedestal and jump high enough to grab hold of the opening, he would never be able to squeeze back through without something supporting his feet.

ShaoShu lowered his head. Unless someone happened to pass by in the next few days, he was doomed.

A soft scraping sound caught his attention, and ShaoShu lifted his head. Was that Tonglong's father's spirit, there to punish him?

He glanced nervously around the darkness and determined that the noise was coming from one corner of the room. He crawled slowly in that direction. As he neared, he figured out what it was. Something was digging.

ShaoShu drew closer to the sound, and he saw that it was only his mouse. He had forgotten all about it. Grateful for the company, he reached out to pick it up. It darted forward, however, quick as a flash, disappearing into the tiny crack it had been pawing at.

ShaoShu pouted. Even his little friend had abandoned him, preferring to hide within the walls. He sighed and lay down to get a closer look at where the mouse was hiding. Perhaps he could coax it out by pretending to have some food.

As he pressed his eye to the crack, ShaoShu uttered a small cry. He could see a faint sliver of moonlight! The crack went clear through to the outside. What's more, the crack appeared to be wider on the outside than on the inside, and the stone floor gave way to dirt in this corner.

ShaoShu recalled what Tonglong had said about a mouse being able to squeeze through any space that could accommodate its head, and he scrambled back over to the pedestal. He felt along the ground until he found what he was looking for—a large, sharp section of the broken urn. He hurried back to the crack and began digging.

It took several hours and many different urn shards, but ShaoShu eventually opened a hole that he could easily slip his head through. In fact, he could have stopped earlier and probably still gotten out, but he didn't feel like dislocating his shoulder again.

By the time he hauled himself out, the sun was beginning to rise. Exhausted and covered with dirt from head to toe, ShaoShu said goodbye to Tonglong's father and dragged himself around to the front of the building. He'd hoped to find a few bites of apple or other offerings left that animals or insects hadn't ravaged. Instead, he was greeted by a sight that made him forget all about his hunger.

"Well, well. Look what the cat dragged in."

ShaoShu frowned. It was Lei.

Tonglong was there, too. He offered ShaoShu a slight bow and said, "Well done, little one. You have impressed me. That is not easy to do."

ShaoShu stared coldly at Tonglong. "You were going to leave me in there, weren't you, sir?"

"Absolutely."

"You are a bad man."

Tonglong grinned. "So I've been told."

ShaoShu turned away, and he heard a slight scurrying sound. He glanced down to see his mouse racing toward him. It hurried up the outside of his pant leg and across his sash, nestling itself deep inside the empty, dirt-laden pouch.

He rested his hand on the pouch, smiling inwardly.

"Isn't that cute," Lei said.

ShaoShu ignored him.

"You have proven yourself, ShaoShu," Tonglong said.

"From this point forward, you are a valuable member of my team." He turned to Lei. "You will keep your cat a respectful distance from ShaoShu and, more importantly, from his mouse, understand?"

Lei bowed. "Yes, sir."

"Good," Tonglong said. "Let us get back to the ship. We shall sail on this morning's tide."

It was late in the day by the time ShaoShu had cleaned the last bits of dirt from behind his ears and beneath his fingernails. This was no easy task with the ship rolling about over heavy seas, but he managed after the cook took pity on him and let him borrow a brush normally reserved for scrubbing potatoes.

Tonglong had told him to be shipshape for a meeting they were going to have that evening. The ship's sailmaker had even made a new robe and pants for ShaoShu out of black silk. He wondered what the meeting could be about, silently hoping that it had nothing to do with his friends. Tonglong's ship had just passed the mouth of the Qiantang River, and he couldn't help but think about Hok and Ying. He'd traveled the river with them.

ShaoShu sighed and looked over at the largest of the treasure piles. Its tarpaulin had been pulled back, and several of Tonglong's men were documenting the items. He had a difficult time comprehending the vast wealth on deck. To him, the shinier an object was, the more it was worth. There sure were a lot of shiny objects there.

He scratched his head, thinking about another shiny object—the key. ShaoShu wondered what it was for.

As his mind continued to wander, Tonglong walked over to him.

"Amazing, isn't it?" Tonglong said. "Most men would give their right arm for only a small portion of this treasure."

ShaoShu shrugged. "I guess, sir." He glanced at the white jade sword Tonglong now wore at his waist. It glowed in the bright afternoon sun.

"Do you like this?" Tonglong asked, gesturing toward the sword. "In many ways, this is worth more than all that treasure combined. Did you know that?"

"Is it worth more than the key, sir?"

Tonglong scowled and lowered his voice. "Never mention the key again. Do you understand?" He gripped the jade sword menacingly.

ShaoShu's eyes widened. "Yes, sir. Understood."

Tonglong pulled the white jade sword out of his sash and examined it. "Doesn't this impress you more than a shiny little key?"

"No, sir."

"Well, it should. And it will. I will have another job for you soon, and acquainting yourself with weapons of every sort is now of the utmost importance."

ShaoShu frowned. "I don't like weapons, sir. They scare me."

"You will learn about them nonetheless, and we shall start right now. This particular sword has almost no value as a weapon in the standard sense, yet it is powerful beyond comprehension. It can sway men's hearts. It is one of four, and many people here and in other regions believe that whoever holds these swords and an accompanying set of white jade armor holds the keys to China's future."

ShaoShu glanced at the small bulge beneath Tonglong's robe, over his heart. It was the key.

Tonglong tapped the key through his robe and leaned close to ShaoShu. "This is the key to *my* future. With the swords, the treasure, and this key, I will be able to succeed where my father failed."

ShaoShu swallowed hard. "What happened to him?"

"My father? He was murdered."

"Murdered! How come, sir?"

"He was too ambitious. Oddly enough, he was done in with the help of someone who was even more ambitious—a traitor from his very own camp. No one knows exactly who the traitor was, but I have my hunches. I will seek my revenge in due time." Tonglong's eyes narrowed. "You're not a traitor, are you, ShaoShu?"

"No, sir!" ShaoShu said, trying to sound as convincing as possible. "What do you want me to do?"

"Spy on someone. Do you think you can do that without getting caught?"

The look on Tonglong's face told ShaoShu that he didn't have a choice. "Yes, sir."

"Good boy," Tonglong said. He shouted across the deck. "Lei!"

Lei hurried over. "Yes, sir?"

"I believe it is time to give ShaoShu a little background about our next project. Tell him about HaiZhe."

"Jellyfish, sir?" ShaoShu asked.

"That's right," Lei said. "HaiZhe is the Southern Warlord, which makes him the most powerful man in this region. I used to work for him, until General Tonglong made me a better offer." Lei grinned, but Tonglong remained stone-faced.

Lei showed ShaoShu a tattoo of a jellyfish that was on his left wrist, and he continued. "The only person higher than a warlord is the Emperor. There are currently three warlords: the Southern Warlord, the Eastern Warlord, and the Western Warlord. The Emperor, who lives in the north, is considered the Northern Warlord. He is by far the most powerful, and the other three warlords send him vast amounts of tribute each month. As long as the warlords keep paying, the Emperor leaves them alone."

"So?" ShaoShu said.

"This has been going on for generations," Lei said. "Nowadays, most of the warlords are merchants first and soldiers second. China has grown weak. HaiZhe here in the south is the worst of the bunch. He has a very strong private force, but his military installations are deplorable. If we were attacked in the south by a foreign force, China would crumble. Tonglong's father figured this out, and he paid the ultimate price for trying to do something about it."

Tonglong's eyebrows rose up. "How did you know about my father?"

Lei cleared his throat and wrung his hands. "Through rumor, I suppose, sir. My humblest apologies if I've offended you."

Tonglong scowled and turned to ShaoShu. "You are just a child, so none of this means anything to you, but I'm sure you've seen the vast number of foreign Round Eyes in the city of Hangzhou. They are here because HaiZhe has grown rich trading with them. However, there are far too many of them, and most are thieving pirates. They've recently taken control of an island less than a day's sail from this very coast, yet HaiZhe does nothing. It is only a matter of time before they take more of our land."

"You want me to spy on HaiZhe, don't you, sir?" ShaoShu asked.

"Do you have a problem with that?"

ShaoShu paused. It sounded dangerous. On the other hand, it had to be far less dangerous than getting on Tonglong's bad side. Besides, perhaps he could somehow use this mission to meet back up with Hok and Ying. "No, sir," ShaoShu replied.

"Excellent," Tonglong said. "Because we've just arrived at his fortress."

ShaoShu looked over at the shore but saw only a sheer cliff that rose as high as a hundred men. He looked closer and noticed a stone staircase, incredibly steep, cut into the cliff. It led from the sea all the way up to a massive stone wall topped with turrets.

A group of men began hurrying down the stairs with what looked like a boat hoisted over their shoulders.

ShaoShu could make out huge black cylinders ringed with a metallic sheen inside the turrets. Cannons—and they were aimed directly at Tonglong's ship.

ShaoShu's nose twitched. He didn't like the looks of this.

"**P**repare to be boarded!" a rough voice called out, and ShaoShu scurried over to the ship's side. The group of men he'd seen on the staircase were now rowing toward Tonglong's vessel. There were four of them. One held a musket that looked battered and in disrepair, even to ShaoShu's untrained eye.

"I'll handle this," Lei said.

ShaoShu turned to see Lei approach with something glowing in his hand. It was a section of slow-burning fuse that the sailors called slow match. ShaoShu had seen great coils of it strategically placed around the ship's deck in metal buckets next to the cannons.

Lei walked over to the side of the ship nearest the

small boat and whipped the cover off one of his immaculate cannons. He angled the great gun down toward the four men and began to lower the fuse over a small hole in the back of the cannon.

One of the men shouted, "Wait!"

"Wait for what?" Lei said. "Wait for you to attempt to shoot me with that rusted excuse for a weapon?"

The man with the musket lowered it. "A thousand pardons, sir. We are only following orders."

"Do you have any idea who commands this vessel?" Lei asked.

Before the man could reply, Tonglong stepped out of his cabin, and ShaoShu's eyes widened.

Tonglong was wearing a magnificent armored jacket made from hundreds of small rectangles of pure white jade stitched together with silk cord. In one hand, he held a white jade sword. In his other hand, he held his straight sword. He approached the side rail, his armor radiant in the evening light.

"General Tonglong!" the man with the musket said. He and the others instantly bowed their heads.

"So, you know of me?" Tonglong asked.

"Of course, sir," the man replied, looking up. "I recognize you from the fight clubs. It is well known that you are also one of the Emperor's top generals. What brings us the honor of your visit?"

"I have come to see HaiZhe."

The men glanced at one another, concern flashing across their faces. "He is not here, sir," one of them said.

"Where is he?"

"He is at his new warehouse in Hangzhou. He lives there now."

Tonglong gave Lei a questioning look.

"It's true," Lei said. "I thought you knew this."

"I did not," Tonglong said, rubbing his chin. "But it does not matter. In fact, it may make things easier." He glared down at the men in the boat, one of whom was murmuring to another.

"What did you say?" Tonglong demanded.

"Your armor, sir," the man replied nervously. "I've heard the legend since I was a boy, but I never dreamed it existed. They say whoever wears it is the rightful ruler of China."

"What do you think?" Tonglong asked.

"Seeing it on the shoulders of someone with your legendary fighting skills, it has to be true."

Tonglong nodded. "So it will be." He turned to Lei, lowering his voice. ShaoShu had to strain his ears to hear what was said.

"How many men does HaiZhe have at this warehouse of his?"

"Roughly one hundred," Lei replied.

"Do they possess cannons and other firearms?"

"They all carry pistols or muskets. HaiZhe also has more than a hundred cannons for sale, but none of them are used for defensive purposes, if that's what you are asking."

"How many soldiers are here in the fortress?"

"Approximately one thousand, I believe."

"Then I've changed my mind," Tonglong said, pulling off his heavy armor. "HaiZhe has abandoned his official post, and I am going to take his command by force. We will keep the jade swords and armor out of sight for now. Is there any chance anyone outside this ship and that small boat knows about them?"

"No, sir," Lei replied. "I've heard talk that some of our men spoke of the treasure to fishermen while we were off paying respects to your father, but to the best of my knowledge, no one mentioned the swords or armor. They probably didn't think anyone would believe them."

"Very well," Tonglong said. "Take these men aboard and add them to our crew. Make sure no one leaves this ship. You and I will take their boat ashore, along with ShaoShu."

"Yes, sir!" Lei said.

ShaoShu stood at the edge of the cliff, overlooking the sea. From up here, he could understand why someone had built a fortress in this location. The stone stairs they'd climbed were on the northernmost edge of an enormous complex that stretched so far to the south it bordered the mouth of the Qiantang River. Someone could easily defend that busy opening from above—that is, if there was anyone posted to defend it.

"This is absurd!" Tonglong said as he turned away from the cliff's edge. "Where *is* everyone?"

"Likely napping or gambling," Lei replied. "Those are their two favorite pastimes."

"Everyone?"

"The men here can bribe their way out of their duties and even their training. Most take advantage of it."

"Who gets the money?"

"Their immediate officers take half. The other half goes to the commander."

Tonglong scowled. "So they only post four men at a time to guard the stairs?"

"Yes, sir. For sentry work, the men prefer to operate in groups of four. That is the ideal number for playing *mahjong*."

Tonglong spat and gazed back over the sea. "This was once the strongest naval base in all China. Where are all the boats?"

"Sold, sir. Or pressed into service as merchant vessels."

"What happened to the docks?"

"A typhoon came through several years ago and destroyed them. At low tide, you can still see a few pilings out there. HaiZhe was going to rebuild but then decided to simply move his operations to Hangzhou. He spent most of his time there, anyway. The river docks are much more convenient than hauling everything up and down these stone stairs."

Tonglong stormed over to one of the cannon turrets. Lei and ShaoShu followed.

"Are these of any use?"

Lei inspected a cannon that had rusted into a fixed position. Beside it sat a pile of lumpy brown metal that appeared to be iron balls fused into a solid mass by years of neglect and decay.

"I might be able to recondition the cannon," Lei said. "But it would take weeks. The shot is of no use to anyone."

"We don't have that kind of time," Tonglong said. "Let's hope their portable equipment has been better maintained. Take us to the encampment."

ShaoShu followed Lei and Tonglong for quite a while before they encountered their first soldier. He was sleeping in a hammock beneath a tree. Tonglong swung his straight sword as they walked past, slicing through the hammock's ropes as though they were nothing more than blades of grass. The man crashed to the ground and jumped to his feet with his hands up, ready for a fight. When he saw Tonglong, he dropped to his knees like a frightened child.

"General Tonglong," the man said. "I recognize you from the fight clubs—"

"Round up the officers," Tonglong ordered, interrupting the man. "Immediately."

The man took off like a shot toward the distant inner compound.

By the time Tonglong, Lei, and ShaoShu arrived at the encampment's series of low buildings, an impressive crowd had gathered. Men were squeezed between the buildings and sitting on the rooftops, elbowing each other for the best viewing spots. They didn't appear to be very disciplined.

Tonglong stopped short of the buildings, and ShaoShu and Lei stayed back several paces. The crowd parted for a fat middle-aged man who strode forward with a confident air, adjusting a ridiculously large hat on his balding head. His robes were brilliant green silk, a stark contrast to the shabby gray cotton uniforms of the men.

"General Tonglong!" the man in green said, offering Tonglong a slight bow. "A pleasure to make your acquaintance. I am Commander Sow."

Tonglong glared at the man, and ShaoShu could almost feel anger flowing from his rigid body. The mouse in his pouch began to squirm.

"You have been neglecting your duty, Commander," Tonglong said tersely. "Your camp is a disgrace."

The commander smiled. "Come now, General. Don't you think you're overreacting?"

"From what I see, you're not prepared for a raid by a handful of schoolchildren, let alone a superior force."

Commander Sow laughed. "Are you alluding to war, sir? We haven't had a war in more than two hundred years! We have no time for war. War is bad for business."

Tonglong's teeth ground loud enough for ShaoShu to hear. "What about the wars in the north?" Tonglong asked. "What about the new Emperor, the man I represent? His inauguration was the result of war."

"We can't concern ourselves with everyone else's business. If we did, who would look after our interests? With all due respect, General, here in the south, one Emperor makes no difference over another. They keep to themselves in the north and leave us alone, and we send them tribute. Boatload upon boatload of tribute, I might add."

"Are you saying that you have no need for an army here?"

"This is a peaceful region," the commander said. "The only difficulties we have are a few pesky bandits by land and the occasional Round Eye pirate by sea."

"Isn't it your duty to stop these Round Eyes?"

"Heavens, no!"

Tonglong's face began to turn a bright red. "Why not?"

The commander looked confused. "Because one of my men might get hurt, of course. No, no. We couldn't have that. What would their families say? We leave the barbarians be. Let them take a shipment here or there. It is a small price to pay for our well-being, don't you think?"

"Would you like to see what I think?" Tonglong asked.

"Nothing would please me more," the commander replied.

ShaoShu watched as Tonglong drew his straight

sword, throwing its ornate scabbard to the ground with unusual force. He gripped the sword's hilt with both hands and twisted his body powerfully from right to left, slicing across Commander Sow's midsection. The sword's blade appeared to have only grazed the commander, but to ShaoShu's dismay, the officer split completely in half. His torso and upper body toppled to one side, while his waist and everything below it fell to the other. Soldiers leaped backward as the air was filled with a shower of red rain.

ShaoShu turned away, shaking violently.

Tonglong glared at the group. "Does anyone here share this man's sentiments?"

Every soldier shook his head.

"Very well," Tonglong said, wiping his blade across the fallen commander's chest. "I blame this buffoon and his absentee leader, HaiZhe, for your regiment's shortcomings. From this moment forward, you have a new commander." He pointed to Lei.

Lei looked surprised, but he bowed respectfully. "At your service, sir!"

Tonglong eyed the soldiers. "Gentlemen, tonight you will go to sleep as commoners. Tomorrow you will wake as warriors. Your new leader is called Commander Lei—Thunder. Some of you might recognize him from the fight clubs. He is going to train you hard for the next several weeks in the repair, maintenance, and use of firearms, while I will drill you in all manner of what it means to be a soldier. No one is to leave this camp. Your next step outside these walls will be as a single fighting unit. Is that clear?"

"Yes, sir!" the men replied as one.

Charles sat at the large table in the apothecary's secret storage room, contemplating his next move. They had arrived without incident, and he was certain no one would ever find him or the others inside this cleverly concealed location. Hok had previously used it as a hideout, and there was more than enough room for them, including Ying, WanSow, Fu, and Malao. However, Charles was concerned about his sloop. If Tonglong and his men had gotten a good look at it while they were at sea, they might be able to identify it. He wanted to get out of there as soon as possible.

"So, what are you going to do?" Hok asked. "We would like you to remain with us, but I understand if you want to be with your friends."

"I'm still not sure," Charles said. "I—"

He was cut short by the seamless hidden door to the room swinging open on silent hinges. It was the apothecary owner, a gentle-looking man called LoBak. As near as Charles could tell, *LoBak* was a respectful way of saying "old man," which was interesting, because the apothecary owner didn't look all that old. He did have thinning gray hair, though, and his wrinkled hands were badly stained a rainbow of colors from years of mixing and grinding medicinal herbs. He closed the door behind him and sat down at the table, handing WanSow a drinking bowl full of steaming liquid.

"What is that?" Hok asked.

"It is the brew I deliver to a local official each night to help him with his . . . condition. It will help her, too. It's a combination of nearly twenty herbs, but the primary ingredient is dragon bone."

Ying's eyebrows raised and he looked at Hok. "Dragon bone? See, I told you it works."

Hok shook her head. "It may very well work, but you are no longer ill, Ying. You take it because you think it makes you more like a dragon."

"You possess dragon bone, Ying?" LoBak asked.

"Enough to last me several years," Ying replied. "Why?"

"You will need it for your mother's treatments. I can supply you with the other ingredients, but dragon bone is difficult to come by, as I'm sure you know."

"You sound as if I will be taking her somewhere," Ying said.

LoBak nodded. "It may be wise for you to leave as soon as she can walk without assistance. The local official I just mentioned is a man called HaiZhe and—"

"Jellyfish!" Fu interrupted.

"That's right," LoBak said. "You know of him?"

"Yes," WanSow said, finishing her drink. "I fear he might soon be looking for me."

"Your fears are well founded," LoBak said. "He has mentioned your name several times. It seems General Tonglong has laid his hands on a veritable dragon's hoard of treasure that HaiZhe has been after for many years. The man giving HaiZhe the news heard about it from a group of fishermen who'd spoken with Tonglong's crew just this morning. They were docked in a village to the south."

"Did they happen to mention a little boy?" Hok asked, her voice anxious. "ShaoShu stowed away on that ship."

"Oh, dear," LoBak said. "ShaoShu did seem a little too curious for his own good while he was here with you. Fortunately, there was no talk of a stowaway. What is he up to?"

"He is trying to help us, I suppose," Hok said. "I was thinking maybe we should stay here in case he happens to sneak away to try and find us. This was the last place I saw him."

"We don't *all* have to stay here," Charles said. "Those of us who can leave should do so."

"But is it safe to leave?" Hok asked. "Now that

HaiZhe knows about the treasure, he'll be searching high and low for it, and for WanSow."

"That's why we should get moving immediately," Charles said.

"I agree with Charles," Fu said.

"What do you think, Malao?" Charles asked.

Malao shrugged. "Don't look at me. None of this sounds like fun."

Charles sniffed. "There is something else we need to consider. What about Tonglong?"

Ying popped his knuckles, one at a time. "Tonglong will get what's coming to him. Trust me."

"What are you going to do?" Charles asked. "No offense, but don't you have other priorities?" He nodded at WanSow.

"I will stay and help WanSow—" Hok began.

"No," Ying said in a firm tone. "I will take care of her myself, and I will deal with Tonglong in time. All of you can do as you see fit."

"Why even worry about going after Tonglong?" Charles said. "I mean, won't the Emperor eventually take care of Tonglong?"

Ying scoffed. "Tonglong works for the Emperor, remember? I am sure the Emperor has no idea what Tonglong is up to. He will build himself into an unstoppable force; then he'll overthrow the Emperor."

"Do you really think so?" Hok asked.

"Count on it," Ying said. "I know Tonglong well. He double-crossed me, and he'll double-cross the Emperor. I think he would even double-cross his mother to get his way."

"Well, somebody has to stop them," Fu growled. "Remember what AnGangseh did to Seh?"

"Look, everyone," Charles said. "This has gotten too big for any of us to handle. Perhaps I should discuss the situation with my friends on Smuggler's Island? You can come with me, if you'd like."

"That might be best," LoBak said. "I know the island you speak of, and it is far more secure than my shop. I suggest all of you leave with Charles when WanSow is ready to travel."

Hok sighed. "I hate to keep imposing on you, Charles, but maybe this would be best. I would like to go with you, and I want to help WanSow. This plan allows for both. Besides, the longer we wait here, the greater the chance we might get word about ShaoShu. What do the rest of you think?"

"Fine with me," Fu said.

"Me too," Malao added.

"Not me," Ying said. "I think you three should go with Charles, but I will take my mother into the mountains to heal where the air is clear and the earth's *chi* is strong. I also have a few things of a personal nature to sort out." He exchanged a knowing look with his mother.

"Are you sure?" Hok asked.

"Yes," Ying said. "I have made some mistakes in the past, and I need to fix them. I am sure our paths will cross again."

"I hope they do," Hok said.

Silence fell over the room.

"Is there anything else we need to discuss?" Charles asked.

No one replied.

"Then it is settled," Charles said. "As soon as WanSow is fit to leave, we shall all be on our way. Now, I suggest we all get some rest. Tomorrow I'd like to start changing the look of my sloop."

The next few weeks were among the most trying of ShaoShu's life. Unable to leave the fortress, he spent nearly all of his time following Lei around like a lost puppy. His orders were to learn as much as possible about firearms in preparation for a future assignment, but without knowing what the assignment was, it was difficult for him to concentrate.

To make matters worse, he had an excellent memory, whereas most of the soldiers did not. Lei had to show the men the same basic tasks over and over before they finally understood the proper way to load a cannon or aim a musket. ShaoShu was certain he could now do these things in his sleep, even though he doubted he ever would. Firearms still frightened him.

Three weeks into the training, things finally began to get interesting. While Tonglong was off drilling a legion of foot soldiers, Lei took ShaoShu and several of the officers out to Tonglong's ship for a demonstration. The cannons aboard were Lei's, and the gun crews were made up of men Lei had previously trained to an extraordinary degree of efficiency. The soldiers and officers on shore had fired numerous muskets and pistols up to that point, but their cannons had remained silent, because the long-neglected weapons had not yet been fully refurbished. So far, their cannon training had involved only practice loading and pretend firing.

There were fourteen cannons on Tonglong's man-o-war, five along each side, plus two at the bow and two at the stern. Lei took command of the centermost cannon along the port side and unlashed it from the ship's side rail with a practiced ease. He ordered the fortress's small transport boat to release six large floating barrels at varying distances from the ship, and once the transport was safely retied to the ship's stern, Lei called all hands to their battle stations.

Amidst a flurry of activity, Lei leaned over, sighting his right eye along the length of his cannon's glimmering bronze barrel. He directed his gun crew to position the cannon to his liking by having them shift the barrel up and down and turn the cannon's carriage side to side on its heavy wooden wheels.

Lei explained that he always left the cannons loaded in case they were attacked, and this particular cannon was packed with a single twelve-pound ball. The floating targets were heavy-duty barrels constructed of wood nearly as thick as the planking on a Chinese junk or a typical Round Eye ship. This exercise would give an accurate representation of what would happen to an enemy vessel in an actual battle.

A gun-crew member lit a section of slow match with a flint firestone and a metal strike bar and handed the slow-burning fuse to Lei. Lei stepped off to one side of the cannon, well away from the bone-crushing undercarriage wheels, and leaned toward the cannon's back end. He timed the roll of the ship in relation to the roll of the targets upon the waves and touched the slow match's burning embers to the cannon's priming hole.

KA-BOOM!

ShaoShu leaped involuntarily at the deafening roar. Flames burst forth from the cannon's barrel, and the carriage recoiled sharply backward on its heavy wheels. Acrid smoke poured out of the cannon, filling half the deck. Across the water, the farthest barrel exploded into a thousand splinters, and the men on deck cheered with delight.

Inside its pouch, ShaoShu's mouse shivered uncontrollably.

Lei barked commands to the other gun crews.

"Men, prepare your guns!"

"Aim your guns!"

"Fire!"

The remaining five barrels were blown out of the

water with alarming accuracy. The entire deck was awash in cannon smoke, and ShaoShu was left half blind and mostly deaf, wondering what Tonglong had in mind for him. He didn't want any part of this.

Hours later, his ears still ringing and his eyes still burning, ShaoShu sat hidden in an empty crate on deck, feeding his mouse. Shouts from high overhead and the sound of men scrambling about on deck drew his attention over the side, where he saw six large Chinese junks approaching. He was worried at first, wondering if the ships were going to attack, but then he realized that the activity on their deck was the sound of men furiously cleaning and straightening after the earlier cannon exercises. They were stowing their great guns, not arming them. No one was going to fire on anyone. ShaoShu breathed a sigh of relief. That is, until Lei called out his name.

"ShaoShu! Where are you hiding now? Meet me in the main cabin at once!"

ShaoShu tucked his mouse into its pouch and hurried to Tonglong's cabin, where he found Lei alone, seated behind Tonglong's desk. ShaoShu considered saying something about Lei being in Tonglong's chair, but then he thought better of it.

"Your time has come," Lei said. "Are you ready?"

ShaoShu frowned. "I think so, sir. It depends on what you want me to do."

"Remember we talked about HaiZhe—Jellyfish?"

ShaoShu nodded. "You want me to spy on him, right?"

"That's right. General Tonglong wants you to collect as much armament information from him as possible, and you're only going to have one night to do it. This isn't going to be easy for you. To be honest, I don't think you'll come out of it alive."

ShaoShu swallowed hard.

"I've been giving this a lot of thought, and it seems to me the most difficult part for you will be sneaking inside the facility itself. Your best chance probably lies with a man called LoBak."

ShaoShu looked at the floor in an effort to try and hide his surprise. He knew exactly who LoBak was. LoBak's shop was the last place he had seen Hok.

"LoBak is an apothecary," Lei continued. "He is a medicine man, and he attends to HaiZhe every evening—he delivers a special drink to help him with his condition."

ShaoShu looked up. "What's wrong with HaiZhe?"

"His legs no longer work. Many years ago, he was a promising young vendor in the local black market. He borrowed money from a group of questionable investors that included, some say, Tonglong's father. When HaiZhe didn't make several loan payments, the investors decided to make an example of him. They severed every tendon in his body from the waist down."

ShaoShu cringed.

"Most people would have died from loss of blood or shock or any number of things," Lei said. "But not HaiZhe. He somehow managed to drag himself down the street to an apothecary, which was how he met LoBak. LoBak has been helping him ever since."

"Does Tonglong know?"

"Of course. HaiZhe's injuries motivated him to crush nearly everyone around him, and he eventually became the Southern Warlord. As I mentioned earlier, Tonglong's father didn't like what he was seeing, and he tried to do something about HaiZhe's ways. Because of this and his presumed role in disabling HaiZhe, some people believe that HaiZhe killed Tonglong's father with the help of a traitor."

"Oh," ShaoShu said, a lump forming in his throat. He couldn't help but think of Tonglong's father's ashes, and he changed the subject. "What about LoBak? Is he HaiZhe's friend?"

"No," Lei said. "LoBak is more like a slave. HaiZhe would kill him if he stopped supplying the medicines that keep him healthy. Wait until you see HaiZhe. He is in amazing shape for someone with his disability."

"How is LoBak going to help me?"

"Indirectly. LoBak always enters through a little-used rear entry that only has one guard. When the guard opens the door for LoBak, you must find a way to sneak in behind him."

ShaoShu closed his eyes. He'd done this sort of thing before, but never with a guard standing there.

"Can you do it?" Lei asked.

ShaoShu opened his eyes and shrugged. "I guess I have no choice."

"Smart boy," Lei said with a grin.

"How will I get to the warehouse?"

Lei pointed out of a porthole to the fortress transport boat tied off at the ship's stern. Workmen swarmed over it, affixing a mast and a sail.

"A group of my best sailors will take you up the river and drop you off at HaiZhe's warehouse," Lei said. "They will use the wind as well as row, as speed is of the essence. Did you notice those six Chinese junks approaching?"

"Yes."

"They are merchant vessels that General Tonglong will use as transports. You may recall that he was gone for a few days last week. That's what he was doing—hiring these captains. He's been planning to mobilize our troops once these ships arrive. The merchant men have no idea what he is up to. Likewise, the men transporting you do not know your true mission. I hope you can keep a secret."

"Sure," ShaoShu said.

"Very good," Lei replied. "The men transporting you will not be wearing uniforms so as to not raise any suspicion. They will drop you off and wait for you. You will only have one night—tonight. Is that clear?"

"Yes," ShaoShu said. "Except, I'm not sure exactly what kind of gun information you want."

"Inventory details. Equipment and supply lists. That is why you have been spending so much time with me. HaiZhe is the largest firearms dealer in China. Nearly all the guns and cannons in our country come from the Round Eyes, and they only work with him. We want to know what he has in his warehouse, including gunpowder and shot."

"Why?"

"So that we can take it, of course. You've seen how pitifully armed we are."

"But once I'm inside, how am I supposed to find it?"

"HaiZhe stores the weapons in a special wing at the eastern end of the building. There is only one doorway in or out, and it's located inside his office. Find the office, and you'll find the door. This will be a challenge, because the doorway into his office is secret. It's hidden within a huge mural down a very long corridor."

Great, ShaoShu thought. *This is going to be impossible.* He said, "If I find a way into the office, how will I know which door is the right one?"

"You can't miss it; it's huge. Be very careful, though, because there is a nearly invisible web of silk trip wires positioned in front of the door. If you so much as breathe too hard on the trip wires, four rows of muskets will simultaneously fire down on you from the ceiling. When I worked for HaiZhe, I saw three different guards accidentally brush against the web. Not even their closest family members could have identified their remains."

"I'm going to die, aren't I?" ShaoShu asked.

"Maybe. I told General Tonglong that I thought this was a bad idea. He said he has faith in you."

ShaoShu stared at Lei. "Tonglong is going to kill HaiZhe, isn't he?"

"With the right kind of information, we might be able to avoid conflict. The last thing General Tonglong wants is a bloody battle in the middle of the city. Perhaps we can pressure HaiZhe into surrendering his position with the information you retrieve, or maybe we can devise a plan to capture the weapons wing with only minimal casualties. If we take control of that wing, HaiZhe will have no choice but to surrender. I have to tell you, though, HaiZhe did not get to be where he is by giving in to pressure. He is as cunning as they come."

Lei turned to the porthole again, and ShaoShu saw the workmen leaving the transport. A mast and sail had been raised, and rugged seamen armed with muskets and pistols were climbing aboard.

"Time for you to go, Little Mouse," Lei said. "Good luck. HaiZhe's life might just be in your hands—as well as your own," he added with a smirk.

CHAPTER 13

ShaoShu's transport vessel sailed hard for hours, the sailors often dropping oars into the water to urge the boat on faster than the sail alone would allow. They were obviously in a hurry, which was fine with ShaoShu. He needed to get there before LoBak's evening visit.

They arrived in front of HaiZhe's warehouse soon after sunset. Most of the merchant ships and smaller transport boats were tied up for the night, bobbing gently in the river's steady current. The sky was overcast, but it didn't look like it was going to rain. ShaoShu couldn't have asked for better conditions. He just hoped they hadn't arrived too late.

He jumped out of the boat and headed for the

enormous warehouse without bothering to say good-bye to Tonglong's men. ShaoShu knew that they would be watching his every move. Or at least as many moves as he would make along the waterfront, which probably wouldn't be many. He was headed around to the back.

As he circled HaiZhe's facility, keeping to the shadows, ShaoShu began to grow anxious. The perimeter was brightly lit with oil lanterns every few paces, and armed guards patrolled the area in random patterns. There was no rhyme or reason to their movements, which meant no weakness for ShaoShu to exploit. He considered trying the roof, but after climbing a tree and looking around, he found that the roof, too, was swarming with guards. Men were stationed within the various roof peaks, armed with muskets. There was no way he or anyone could get inside there without being noticed. These guards were very different from the soldiers at the fortress.

As ShaoShu shimmied down the tree, he heard someone approaching. He dove beneath a small evergreen and watched a well-worn path that led to one of the building's back doors.

An older man came strolling up the path toward the warehouse, carrying a drinking bowl filled with a steaming liquid. ShaoShu smiled. It was LoBak. As LoBak neared his hiding place, ShaoShu whispered, "*Psst!* LoBak! Mr. Medicine Man! Down here! It's me, ShaoShu—Hok's friend!"

LoBak slowed but did not stop. He kept his eyes fixed straight ahead and whispered out of the corner of his mouth, "Lower your head and cover your face."

ShaoShu was about to ask why when LoBak appeared to stumble. ShaoShu ducked as instructed, and the last thing he saw was LoBak twist around and fling the drinking bowl in his direction. ShaoShu bit his lip as the scalding liquid splashed over the evergreen branches onto him. He didn't cry out, though. Not even when the drinking bowl bounced off the side of his head.

"Oh, dear," LoBak said loudly to no one in particular. "I shall have to make another batch. Now, where did my drinking bowl go?" He bent down and stuck his face into the tree.

"What are you doing here?" LoBak asked in a low whisper. "I heard that you were with Tonglong. Come with me. Hok and Ying are hiding at my shop."

ShaoShu frowned. "I can't leave. I have to sneak into HaiZhe's warehouse, or Tonglong will kill me."

LoBak sighed. "You poor thing. You will never get in there without help. Wait here, I'll be back soon." He grabbed the drinking bowl and left, calling out to the guards, "I will return shortly. Pass the word to Warlord HaiZhe about my spill."

Half an hour later, LoBak returned with a rigid basket strapped to his back and a canteen slung around his neck. He set the basket down next to ShaoShu's evergreen tree and removed the lid, whispering, "Hok and Ying send their greetings. I nearly had to threaten their lives to keep them from coming with me. Hok tells me that you can squeeze into tight spaces. Is this true?"

"Yes."

"Excellent. When you hear me cough, climb into the very bottom of this basket."

"Okay."

LoBak reached into the basket and pulled out a small saw and a large blanket. He carried the items well away from ShaoShu and began to saw a branch from a cypress tree.

"You there, Medicine Man!" a guard shouted from the rooftop. "What do you think you are doing?"

LoBak coughed, and ShaoShu scrambled into the basket headfirst. He heard LoBak say, "I am preparing a special treatment for Warlord HaiZhe using his very own trees. Would you like to come down and help?"

"I cannot, sir," the guard replied. "I need to remain at my post. Carry on."

LoBak did carry on. He cut three branches from the tree and carried them back to the basket. ShaoShu was settled in by then, having twisted and squirmed his body into a tight knot, barely taking up any space at the bottom of the basket.

"Amazing," LoBak whispered.

ShaoShu mumbled, "Thanks," into his right ankle, which was pressed against his mouth.

LoBak draped the blanket over ShaoShu, set

the saw and cypress branches gently on top, and closed the lid. Then he hoisted the basket onto his back, adjusted the canteen around his neck, and walked through the back door, into HaiZhe's secret world.

CHAPTER 14

"**H**alt!" a voice commanded as soon as LoBak stepped through HaiZhe's back door. "Who goes there?"

Oh, no, ShaoShu thought from the bottom of the basket. *Have we been found out already?*

"It is the apothecary," LoBak replied. "I am here to administer Warlord HaiZhe's treatment."

"You're late," the guard said. "I'd advise you to watch your step next time. You know how he is about keeping schedules."

"Yes, sir," LoBak replied.

ShaoShu felt LoBak begin to walk again, and he shifted his contorted body until he could peer out of a tiny gap in the basket's tightly woven sides. He saw that they were in a wide corridor lit with small oil lanterns similar to the lanterns outside. LoBak weaved through numerous hallways, and they passed two more guard stations before stopping in front of a gigantic mural that stretched as far down the corridor as ShaoShu could see. Thousands of meticulously painted jellyfish swarmed the walls, their swaying limbs stinging everything in their path with emotionless ferocity. His nose twitched. This was a very bad place.

LoBak pressed his hand against a particularly large jellyfish, and a section of the wall swung open. There was no way ShaoShu would have found that alone. He thanked the heavens for LoBak.

"Do you know what time it is?" asked a gruff voice from within the next room.

"Sorry I'm late, sir," LoBak replied, walking through the opening and closing the secret door behind him. "I sent word, and I hoped that you would be notified. I had to make your preparation twice. Also, I've learned of a new treatment you might want to consider. It took me a while to find just the right elements."

"I am content with my current treatment," HaiZhe grumbled.

"I will administer that as well, sir," LoBak said, knocking against the canteen strung around his neck. "I'll bring it over to you."

ShaoShu felt LoBak shrug the basket off his back and place it on the floor. From this new angle,

ShaoShu had a clear view of HaiZhe sitting behind a large desk. He didn't look like he had any sort of disability, appearing as healthy as any man could. He was perhaps fifty-five years old and had a head full of thick white hair, wide powerful shoulders, and rather large arms. Strapped to each of his upper arms was a holster, and in each holster was a pistol. By ShaoShu's account, none of this added up to the nickname "Jellyfish."

LoBak placed the canteen on HaiZhe's desk and opened it. HaiZhe took several long drinks of the steaming liquid, then looked over at the basket.

"What's in there?"

"Cypress boughs," LoBak replied. "That is the new treatment. I've just spoken with a colleague who swears that sleeping on them improves circulation."

"Let me take a look."

"No, no," LoBak replied, hurrying back to the basket. "I'll get them for you. They are rather large and awkward, and—"

"I will do it myself!" HaiZhe snapped. "Do you think me incapable?"

HaiZhe pushed his chair away from the desk and leaned sideways, disappearing from view. A moment later, he reappeared on the floor, on his stomach. He crawled toward the basket using only his hands and upper body, his withered legs dragging behind him like wet noodles.

ShaoShu shuddered. He felt bad for HaiZhe.

As HaiZhe neared, ShaoShu turned his eyes away

from the gap in the basket and held his breath. He heard HaiZhe grunt, and the lid flew off the basket. ShaoShu felt the branches being lifted off of him, followed by the saw.

"What is this?" HaiZhe asked, shaking the saw so hard its metal blade sang out. "You know better than to bring a weapon into my inner sanctum."

"Sorry, sir," LoBak replied. "I suppose I didn't consider it a threat against anything except trees. I won't let it happen again."

"Don't get smart with me," HaiZhe warned. He threw the saw back into the basket, and the impact caught ShaoShu by surprise. He managed to remain silent, but his mouse let out a tiny squeak.

ShaoShu held his breath.

Nothing happened. HaiZhe coughed with an authoritative dismissal and dragged himself away with the cypress boughs in tow.

ShaoShu breathed easy again.

"I should like to set those up for you," LoBak called after HaiZhe.

"I will do it myself."

"With all due respect, sir," LoBak said, "I have knowledge concerning the correct placement. At least let me check to make sure they're arranged properly."

"You certainly are a pest," HaiZhe replied. "But your judgment is usually sound. I will summon you once I am finished. Wait here until you are called. Be prepared to spend the night, too. If this new treatment interferes with my sleep, I plan to beat you with the main ingredients."

ShaoShu heard a door open and then close. The next instant, the blanket was lifted and LoBak was standing over him with a worried look on his face. ShaoShu suddenly didn't feel bad for HaiZhe anymore.

"I'm really sorry," ShaoShu whispered as he stood and stretched. "I hope HaiZhe doesn't beat you."

"He won't," LoBak replied. "The cypress bough treatment is authentic. I've been meaning to have him try it for some time."

ShaoShu glanced about HaiZhe's private office. He expected to see opulent surroundings, but the only furnishings were the large desk and chair and several oil lanterns along the walls to provide light in the windowless room. The only decoration was another jellyfish mural that marked the secret door. There were also two regular doors, one of average size across the room to ShaoShu's right and a larger one to his left, in a corner.

"I have to be honest with you," LoBak whispered. "I don't like the way things are shaping up. I am not sure I can get you back out of here in that basket."

"That's okay," ShaoShu said. "I didn't want to have to squeeze in there again, anyway. I can find my own way out."

"That is easier said than done. The hidden door we used to get in here is the only way in or out." LoBak pointed to the small door. "That one leads to

HaiZhe's private living quarters, while the larger one leads to the warehouse's weapons wing. Neither space has any windows or additional doors. I should never have brought you here."

"I'll be fine," ShaoShu said. "I'll just hide with the weapons and climb into something that is being loaded out. Are you sure everything passes through that one door?"

"Positive. HaiZhe believes it is more secure that way. Only his most trusted men are allowed to load and unload the stock, and the door is rigged with a trap that only he knows how to disarm."

"I heard about the trap. I think—"

"LoBak!" HaiZhe called out from behind the small door. "Get in here and perform your inspection! I have work to do yet tonight."

LoBak's expression changed to one of genuine concern, and ShaoShu whispered, "I'll be okay. Tell Hok and Ying I'll see them soon."

LoBak mouthed, "Good luck," and he headed for HaiZhe's private quarters. Once LoBak entered and closed the door behind him, ShaoShu carefully approached the larger door in the opposite corner.

The large door was hung so that it swung away from HaiZhe's office, into the weapons wing. It had been left slightly ajar, as if tempting a passerby to peek through it. ShaoShu looked high and low but saw no sign of trip wires. He reached up and took a small lantern from the wall, playing the flickering flame across the corner while watching from one side. In the sidelight, the silk threads showed themselves. They were woven together about two paces in front of the door, with only a small narrow space left open along the floor that no normal person could possibly pass through.

ShaoShu, however, was far from normal. He memorized the layout of the trip wires nearest the floor, then hung the lantern back on the wall. He dropped to the ground in front of the web and lay down on his back, taking several deep breaths before exhaling forcefully to deflate his chest. He turned his head to one side and slid headfirst beneath the web, pushing with his feet.

His upper body made it through. Once his waist cleared, ShaoShu sat up and wiggled backward on his butt until his legs were through, too. Sitting up, he carefully peeked through the open door and saw that the cavernous space beyond was dimly lit with lanterns on the walls. He scanned the weapons wing as best he could and didn't see anyone.

ShaoShu took a deep breath and stood, keeping well clear of the trip wires. He gave the large door a gentle push, and it swung open easily and silently on well-oiled hinges. He slipped inside, nudging the door back toward its original position. Unfortunately, the door moved far too easily. Before ShaoShu could react, it closed completely with a barely audible *click*. He grabbed the handle and tried to open it, but it was locked.

There was no turning back now. Hopefully, no one would notice that the door had closed.

It took a few moments for his eyes to fully adjust to the dim light, but when they did, ShaoShu's mouth dropped open in awe.

Along one entire side of the wing, barrels of gunpowder and crates of shot were stacked in organized piles, many reaching the ceiling. Mounds of wadding and stacks of ramrods formed a neat barrier between the gunpowder and the weapons themselves, aligned along the opposing wall. The armaments were sectioned off into distinct groups that made sense even to ShaoShu. The huge room was filled to capacity with every type of musket, cannon, and pistol he had ever seen. There were many devices he didn't recognize, though their numerous powder burns and thick metal sides made it clear they were weapons of war. ShaoShu tried his best to make a mental image of everything he saw.

Like LoBak had said, this room had no windows and only one door. Beside the door stood a desk, upon which rested four scrolls. ShaoShu walked over and opened one. He guessed it was some sort of inventory list. Rows of writing corresponded with columns of numbers, filling the entire page. As he turned it over in his hands, he smiled. This was exactly what he was looking for.

His happiness was short-lived, however. On the far side of the door, ShaoShu heard voices. He leaned his ear to it and listened as two guards debated whether they should interrupt HaiZhe about some tiny foot-

prints they had found beneath a small evergreen behind the warehouse. One of them noticed that the
weapons wing door was closed, and as they discussed
whether this was noteworthy, ShaoShu decided he
needed to find a way out of there immediately. He
shoved the inventory scrolls into his sash and raced
away from the door, keeping to the wall nearest the
armaments.

More than halfway down the length of the wall,
ShaoShu nearly stumbled over a small barrel of gunpowder that someone must have misplaced. It should
have been on the opposite side of the room, but it
gave him an idea. Lei had once shown him and the
soldiers how to make a bomb with nothing more than
a barrel of gunpowder and a fuse. It was easy. What's
more, he realized that with a little bit of effort, he
might be able to blast a hole in the wall and make it
look like an accident.

ShaoShu nudged the small barrel against the
wall below one of the lanterns and reached up, lift-
ing the lantern's protective glass. He blew out the
flame, took the lantern off the wall, and laid it on
top of the barrel. He wanted to make it look as if the
lantern had fallen and ignited the misplaced barrel
of powder. He had no idea what would remain of
the lantern or the barrel, but he hoped there would
be enough clues left for HaiZhe to believe what he
wanted him to believe.

ShaoShu found two short sections of slow match
nearby, and he uncorked the barrel. He carefully set

one piece of slow match into the gunpowder keg, then walked over to a different lantern and set the second section of slow match alight. His hands shaking, ShaoShu headed back to the barrel. He lit the first piece of slow match, dropped the second one, and ran.

KA-BOOM!

The barrel exploded with unbelievable force a few moments after ShaoShu took cover behind a massive cannon. Even with the big gun protecting him, he was rocked back on his heels. Thick smoke filled his lungs, and he waved it frantically away, trying not to cough. He gazed over at the wall and saw a small hole and several deep cracks in the brickwork at floor level. An adult could never fit through that opening, but he could.

ShaoShu headed for the hole, wriggling through it as HaiZhe began to shout orders from the opposite side of the large door. ShaoShu hit the ground running outside and checked his sash. The scrolls were still there, as was his mouse's pouch. He glanced around and saw that he'd exited on the front side of the building. He expected to encounter guards, but they'd all left their posts. They were flooding into the main entrance, shouting to one another about the explosion. They had no idea he was there.

ShaoShu considered trying to find LoBak's apothecary shop to see Hok and Ying, but through the ringing in his ears, he heard Tonglong's men shouting to him from the riverfront. He looked over and saw them gesturing excitedly. They wanted to leave.

One of Tonglong's soldiers raised a musket in his direction. It was a threat. Hok and Ying would have to wait. He hurried into the boat and nestled himself beneath an old tarpaulin, and the men shoved off.

CHAPTER 15

ShaoShu yawned as he stood in front of Tonglong and Lei many hours later. He was covered from head to toe with smoke and gunpowder stains, but he had completed his mission successfully. After some rest, he hoped to come up with a plan to reunite with Hok and Ying, and hopefully to rescue LoBak. For now, he held out the four inventory scrolls that had nearly cost him his life.

"Well done!" Tonglong said, taking the scrolls. He unrolled the first one, and a confused look crossed his face. He unrolled the second and the third, and finally the fourth.

In a fury, Tonglong hurled the first three scrolls across the room, holding up the fourth for ShaoShu to see.

"Did you even bother to look at these?" Tonglong asked.

"Yes, sir," ShaoShu replied. "I looked at one."

"Which one?"

ShaoShu leaned forward and inspected the scroll in Tonglong's hand. "That one."

"Are you certain?"

"I think so, sir."

Tonglong's cold eyes burned with rage. "What does it say?"

"It's full of numbers and characters. Words, sir."

"What words?"

ShaoShu shrugged, tears filling his eyes. "I don't know! I'm sorry, sir! I can't read."

Tonglong threw the scroll against the wall. "That one is a list of women's undergarments! Why didn't you tell me you couldn't read?"

ShaoShu saw Lei laughing silently next to Tonglong and lowered his head. "I'm an orphan, sir. I never went to school."

"Get out of my sight!" Tonglong roared. "You are to remain in your quarters indefinitely."

ShaoShu looked up. *Indefinitely?* He would never be able to get back to Hok and Ying if he was stuck in his quarters.

"But, sir," ShaoShu said, his mind racing, "I can still be of use. I saw a lot of things, and I have a great memory. If you come with me to the shed where Lei keeps the guns and cannons, I think I can tell you how many of each I saw."

Tonglong glowered at him. "Are you certain?"

"I'd bet my life on it, sir."

"I'll take that bet," Tonglong said, standing. "You will not fail me again."

An hour later, ShaoShu stood between Lei and Tonglong, pointing to items and providing quantities faster than Lei could write them down. Lei filled a full inventory scroll before ShaoShu said, "I think that's it, sir."

Lei put his writing brush down and grinned. "Not bad, for a kid."

Tonglong nodded. "Not bad at all, assuming he is correct. Let's see what else he remembers."

"Sir?" ShaoShu said.

"Tell us about the warehouse and the weapons wing," Tonglong said. "You never explained how you managed to sneak in there."

ShaoShu thought for a moment. He didn't want Tonglong or Lei to know that he already knew LoBak. "I followed LoBak, the apothecary owner, inside."

"The apothecary owner?" Tonglong asked.

"LoBak administers treatments to HaiZhe every night," Lei said. "I suggested ShaoShu use that to his advantage." He turned to ShaoShu. "What about the secret door to HaiZhe's private quarters and the guard stations along the way?"

"The guards were easy to sneak past," ShaoShu said. "Inside, they were always in pairs, and they spent most of their time talking instead of watching the hallways. I saw LoBak push a special jellyfish on a big mural to open the secret door, and I waited a little while before copying him. I got lucky that no one was in the office when I snuck in. I couldn't have done it without you. Thanks for telling me about the trap—"

"That is excellent," Lei interrupted. "You are most welcome."

Tonglong nodded, seemingly satisfied. "I've been told that you exited the facility by blasting a hole in the warehouse exterior."

"Yes, sir," ShaoShu said. "There was only one exit out of HaiZhe's weapons wing, and it was back through the office that was blocked by guards. I had to make my own little door." He smiled.

Lei chuckled. "You certainly are something else, ShaoShu."

Tonglong rubbed his chin. "Are you saying that the weapons wing is enclosed by an exterior wall, and you blasted through it without blowing up the entire warehouse?"

"Yes, sir. The gunpowder is stored against a different wall, far away. There are also many rows of things between the wall I blasted and the gunpowder barrels."

"I see," Tonglong said. "Is it true that the hole you made was in the front of the building, facing the river?"

"Yes, sir."

"What size charge did you use?"

"I don't know. It was a small barrel of black powder about this big." ShaoShu held up both hands to show the size. "I don't see one here, but I believe I've heard Lei call it a powder keg."

Tonglong nodded. "What sort of material was the wall made of?"

"Brick, sir."

Tonglong grinned.

"Are you thinking what I'm thinking?" Lei asked.

Tonglong's grin grew into a wide smile. "Forget negotiations. ShaoShu has solved the problem of how we can get in."

ShaoShu found himself back aboard another boat before the sun was even halfway across the sky. This time, it was Tonglong's man-o-war. He rubbed his weary eyes and stared at the crowded shore, half-asleep despite the brisk autumn breeze blowing hard against his face. He'd remained on deck because he hoped to slip away the moment they landed. He missed Hok and Ying tremendously.

HaiZhe's warehouse came into view, and Tonglong roared, "Battle stations!"

ShaoShu quickly backed away from the rail as men swarmed the cannons along that side of the ship. The great guns had already been primed and loaded to Lei's exact specifications based on Tonglong's requirements.

"Remember to mind the recoil, gentlemen!" Lei said as he paced the deck. "With these loads, they'll kick like mules. Untie the carriages!"

Two men from each cannon team released the thick ropes that secured the cannons and their wheeled platforms to the deck and side rail. The two remaining team members at each cannon kept their eyes glued to the shore, awaiting further instructions.

ShaoShu followed their gaze and saw guards scrambling in front of HaiZhe's warehouse. They knew something was amiss. It wasn't every day they saw a man-o-war pulling up broadside in front of their facility, not to mention one with the six merchant ships in its wake, each packed to its topmasts with soldiers.

ShaoShu looked up at the four gigantic sails on Tonglong's ship. Like the merchant vessels, the sails had rigid bamboo slats positioned parallel to the water that ran from the sail's wide bottom all the way up to its narrow top. The slats were intended to keep the sail open and were strung close enough for men to climb them like a ladder so they could reach the upper rigging. Soldiers on Tonglong's ship clambered up the slats, long-range pistols tucked into the folds of their robes.

HaiZhe had a great many armed guards, but they would be no match for Tonglong's shipload of men. And when you factored in the thousand soldiers in the merchant vessels armed with swords and spears, HaiZhe didn't stand a chance.

Tonglong suddenly shouted, "Fire at will, Commander!"

"Aye, aye, General!" Lei shouted back. In a thundering voice, he continued. "On my mark, men! Aim for the northernmost corner of the building. One shot per cannon. We only want to break through the wall, not demolish it. Ready . . . aim . . . FIRE!"

ShaoShu jammed his fingers into his ears and dropped to his knees. The ship rocked violently as cannons roared along its length. His mouse shuddered terribly in its pouch, and smoke thicker than he'd ever imagined blocked out the sun. When it finally began to clear, ShaoShu stood.

He looked toward shore. Several gaping holes were clearly visible in the side of the warehouse, and he could see guards moving about inside. One man ran outside, carrying a flag attached to a staff. The flag was embroidered with a jellyfish. The man rammed the staff into the ground and dropped to his knees, kowtowing three times in the direction of the ship.

ShaoShu hurried over to Lei. "What is he doing?"

"Surrendering," Lei said with a satisfied grin.

"Commander Lei!" Tonglong shouted. "I am going ashore with a group of men. Remain here with the ships."

"Aye, aye, General," Lei replied.

Tonglong's man-o-war eased into a gigantic dock, and Tonglong leaped ashore, followed by more than fifty armed soldiers. The merchant vessels began to dock, too, a thousand men ready to storm the warehouse if Tonglong should command it.

As Tonglong neared the facility, Lei walked over to one of the sails and began to climb, presumably to get a better view. ShaoShu decided this was his chance to escape. He lifted one leg over the side rail and heard a loud "Meow!"

ShaoShu froze.

From behind, halfway up the sail, ShaoShu heard Lei ask, "Where do you think you are going?"

"To see if I can help General Tonglong," ShaoShu said quickly. "I was in there before, remember?"

After a moment, Lei said, "All right. But I will be watching you."

"Yes, sir," ShaoShu replied. He scrambled over the side and jumped down to the wooden dock, running straight toward the warehouse. Tonglong had just entered, and several soldiers were already posted outside the gaping holes. None of them stopped ShaoShu.

ShaoShu passed through the warehouse wall in time to see HaiZhe's guards lay down their weapons. There were perhaps fifty, and they kowtowed in unison, each knocking his forehead against the floor three times.

"You may rise," Tonglong said. "And you may keep your weapons. You will need them. You all work for me now, and we have work to do."

The guards looked up with blank, confused faces, and HaiZhe called out from the far side of the large door, which was wide open. "Do as he says, men. It appears as though my time as your Southern Warlord has come to an end. General Tonglong, would you be so kind as to come here and collect my pistols as proof of my submission to your superior force?"

Tonglong's eyes narrowed, and he stared at HaiZhe lying on the floor, his useless legs splayed out behind him.

HaiZhe removed his pistols and set them down, then backed away until he was out of ShaoShu's sight.

Tonglong headed for the doorway, and ShaoShu remembered the trip wires. "General Tonglong, wait!" he called out. "It's a trap! HaiZhe has silk strings connected to muskets in the ceiling."

Tonglong stopped. "What are you doing here, ShaoShu?"

"I came to see if I could help, and I'm glad I did, sir. Commander Lei cut me off before I could tell you about the trap. I had to sneak beneath it, or I would have been blown to bits."

HaiZhe laughed. "That little rat can't be trusted. Come into my office, General, and let me tell you about my old friend LoBak."

Tonglong took a step forward, and ShaoShu sprang into action. He grabbed a bag of musket balls and headed for Tonglong, hurling the bag through the doorway.

KA-POW! POW! POW! POW!

Musket shot rained down from the ceiling, ricocheting off the floor and walls. Thick smoke billowed through the doorway.

Tonglong's face hardened, and ShaoShu stared beyond him, through the doorway. From this angle, ShaoShu saw LoBak, bound and gagged, lying next to HaiZhe. Neither appeared to have been injured by the musket fire.

HaiZhe reached for his pistols.

BANG!

HaiZhe's body suddenly lurched backward and went limp, lying still. ShaoShu turned to see Lei holding a smoking pistol, a huge grin on his face.

"Congratulations, General Tonglong," Lei said. "You are now officially the Southern Warlord."

Tonglong spun around. "I thought I told you to stay with the ship!?" he said angrily.

"And miss all the fun?" Lei replied. "Not a chance."

Tonglong scowled. "I would have preferred to take HaiZhe alive. How long have you been standing there?"

"Long enough to know what I had to do, sir. I am sorry if you feel I did the wrong thing. It won't happen again."

Tonglong cursed, walking away toward his new soldiers and the huge stockpile of gunpowder barrels against the far wall.

Lei headed for ShaoShu. "Why did you say that I cut you off before you could tell General Tonglong about the trip wires?"

"I . . . I don't know," ShaoShu replied nervously.

"You had better watch your back, Little Mouse," Lei said, tapping the pistols across his chest. "Accidents happen all the time with guns around."

ShaoShu swallowed hard, and Lei breezed past him into HaiZhe's office. Lei hauled LoBak to his feet. "You're coming with me, Medicine Man," he said. "You know too much about HaiZhe's operations to be running loose."

ShaoShu followed them back to the docks, where Lei handed LoBak off to a group of sailors. "Take him below," Lei said. "I shall return shortly."

"Aye, sir," the sailors replied.

Lei turned to ShaoShu. "Get on the boat and stay

there. If you step out of line, you will join the old man in the hold. Is that clear?"

"Yes, sir," ShaoShu said.

Lei hurried back to the warehouse, and ShaoShu climbed aboard Tonglong's man-o-war. He considered trying to sneak belowdecks to check on LoBak but decided not to risk it. At least, not yet.

Bored, ShaoShu scurried up one of the ship's tall sails. He found it remarkably easy to do with the bamboo slats. Stopping near the top, he surveyed the surroundings. From this vantage point, he could see all around HaiZhe's warehouse. Soldiers and sailors were busy removing items from the weapons wing, transporting them to Tonglong's ship and the six merchant vessels. They were making quick work of it.

After some time, Lei returned with a box under his arm. He entered Tonglong's cabin and emerged a quarter of an hour later with the box, plus a small scroll. Lei was blowing on the scroll's wax seal to cool it down, and ShaoShu noticed that he was now wearing a large ring. It was shiny, so it caught ShaoShu's attention. He strained his eyes and saw that the ring had a raised image on top. ShaoShu knew that these types of rings were used to imprint a special pattern or design into a wax seal as a private signal. The image on this ring matched the image imprinted in the wax on the scroll. Even from where he rested, ShaoShu could see that the image was a cobra.

Lei seemed to suddenly remember that he was wearing the ring and slipped it into one of his holster pouches. He glanced around and then up. His eyes met ShaoShu's, and Lei's face darkened. He slid the scroll into the folds of his robe and ordered ShaoShu down.

ShaoShu stepped onto the deck, and Lei seized his elbow. "I warned you to keep your nose out of my business, Little Mouse," Lei said in a harsh whisper. "You're coming with me. General Tonglong will be so busy the next few days, he won't even miss you. I am going to show you how a sailor ties knots. Your contortionist tricks will get you nowhere on my watch."

CHAPTER 16

ShaoShu sat propped beside LoBak in the hold of Tonglong's ship, surround by crates of cannonballs. He had never been tied up so tightly or so thoroughly. Complex knots held his arms pinned to his sides with rope that didn't have the slightest stretch. No matter how much he tried to twist or turn or expand or compress his body, the bindings did not give.

He sighed and closed his eyes. Above his head, he heard the sound of cannons being repositioned on deck and Lei's strong voice shouting orders. The boats were fully loaded and the men were being pressed to set sail as soon as possible in order to make another attack. It seemed Tonglong was eager to put his new power to use.

ShaoShu opened his eyes and turned to LoBak, whose gag had been removed by one of the kinder sailors. So far, nobody suspected that he and LoBak knew each other.

"I am so sorry," ShaoShu said. "I should never have asked you to help me."

"Do not say such things," LoBak replied in a brittle voice. "I knew what was at risk, even if you did not. Men like HaiZhe, Tonglong, and Lei are not to be trifled with. We should consider ourselves fortunate we are still breathing. You, especially."

ShaoShu frowned. "I wish I could have snuck off this ship when we first landed. I had planned to run to your shop to get Ying and Hok. They would know what to do."

"That would have proved fruitless. They are gone. We agreed that if I did not return within a few hours, something was amiss and they were to leave before first light. I am sure they were well on their way before this vessel even made it to the mouth of the Qiantang River."

ShaoShu breathed a sigh of relief. "That's good. Where did they go?"

"Ying was to take his mother to the mountains, while Hok was to accompany her temple brothers Fu and Malao to a nearby island with a Round Eye called Charles. They will be staying in a place known as Smuggler's Island, which is home to a large band of very rough foreigners. We had agreed that this was the best plan, but now I have my doubts."

"What do you mean?" ShaoShu asked.

"I overheard sailors talking as they loaded this hold. They spoke of reports about a group of Round Eye pirate ships traveling south together just this morning. They think the boats came from Smuggler's Island, and Tonglong means to attack the island's stronghold cove while it is shorthanded."

"Oh, no!" ShaoShu whispered. "Tonglong *hates* foreigners! I wish there was something we could do to warn them." Frustrated, he struggled and strained against his bindings one more time, but it was no use. He made no headway whatsoever. Tired, he leaned back against a cannonball crate.

Something began to stir next to ShaoShu's belly button, and he held his breath. At first it felt like a mosquito, but then it began to tickle. Unable to control himself, he giggled softly.

"This is no laughing matter," LoBak said.

"Sorry, sir," ShaoShu said. "It's my mouse. He lives in a pouch attached to my sash. When Lei tied me up, he must have forgotten about it. He wrapped the ropes right over the pouch. I don't think my mouse likes it. He's squirming around, trying to get out. It tickles."

ShaoShu sucked in his stomach to give the mouse a little more room, and it stopped squirming. However, its lack of motion was replaced with something else—the sound of tiny teeth gnashing together.

"Hey!" ShaoShu whispered. "He's trying to chew his way out!"

LoBak glanced at ShaoShu's ropes. "Are you sure?"
ShaoShu nodded.

"It looks like your major bindings converge right over your midsection," LoBak said. "If he makes it all the way through, there is a good chance you might be able to wriggle free!"

ShaoShu grinned. "That's exactly what I was thinking."

CHAPTER 17

"Ahoy, friend!" Charles shouted in Dutch to the fishing boat drifting across the mouth of Smuggler's Island cove. "Permission to enter your sheltered waters?"

"Why, Charles!" one of the fishermen replied in the same language. "What have you done to your sloop? Come in! Come in!"

Charles steered his newly changed sloop toward the cove's calm waters in the fading daylight. He'd modified his boat's rigging so much and painted it such a different color that even he had a hard time recognizing it.

The fishing boat gave way, and the fishermen began hoisting several flags in quick succession. Charles waved to the man who'd greeted him, and while he recognized his face, he didn't recall his name. Nor could he interpret the signal flag messages that were flying up and down the fishing boat's mast.

It had been a while since Charles had had to interpret signal flags, but he should have been able to decipher at least some of the message. The fact that he couldn't meant that Captain Henrik wasn't there. Someone else was in charge.

As Charles' sloop slipped through the cove, he saw only one ship moored there—a schooner that belonged to a Captain Rutger. No other boats were in sight, which was odd. Charles had never seen fewer than three ships in the cove at any one time. Usually there were five or more.

Hok walked over to his side. "Is everything all right? You look concerned."

"Everything is fine," Charles replied.

Hok scanned their surroundings and pointed toward the vessel patrolling the mouth of the cove. "That's not really a fishing boat, is it?"

"Sure it is," Charles said. "They're trolling for tomorrow's breakfast. Fish like to inhabit the narrow breakwater where the cove meets the ocean. As you've guessed, the fishermen are also sentries. They are the first line of defense in case there is an attack." He pointed to a cluster of trees on each side of the cove's rocky mouth. "The second line of defense is the cannons positioned in those two tree groupings. If the fishermen were to give the signal, we would be blown out of the water."

Hok nodded and looked back at him, staring with unblinking eyes.

"What?" he asked.

"There is something troubling you. I can sense it. I thought you would be happy to be back among your friends."

"I am happy," Charles said. "Sort of. I didn't say anything earlier because I didn't want to get your hopes up, but I had thought your father, Captain Henrik, would be here. I thought his crew would be, too. My crew."

Hok continued to stare at him, her expression unchanged.

"I am certain he is not here, though," Charles went on. "His ship is not in the cove, and they aren't

using his signal book. Another captain is in charge right now. Captain Rutger is a good man. You'll like him."

Hok looked away, over the side. "I remember you once told me that my father was conducting business in the south. I guess I hoped he would be here, too. Sometimes I wonder if I'll ever see him again."

"We'll know more after we talk with Captain Rutger. Look, there he is, aboard his schooner."

Charles pointed to a slender man in his forties with bright intelligent eyes. He had brown hair, broad shoulders, and a strong chin. He stood like a rock, grinning, upon the poop deck.

"Ahoy, Captain Rutger!" Charles called out in Dutch. "Permission to come aboard?"

"Charles!" Captain Rutger replied in Chinese with a warm laugh. "Permission granted! A hearty welcome to you and your mates!"

Charles glanced back at Fu in the stern, then up at Malao in the rigging. "We're going to tie off to that large boat," Charles said. "Prepare to drop sail on my mark. Ready . . . and . . . release sheets!"

Fu and Malao raced about, lowering the sails with seaman-like precision. Charles expertly steered his sloop alongside the schooner, the sides of the vessels bumping gently, and Captain Rutger dropped them a line. Charles tied off his boat and climbed aboard the schooner, followed by Hok, Malao, and Fu.

"Welcome aboard," Captain Rutger said in perfect Mandarin. "Any friends of Charles' are friends of mine. To make things more comfortable, I shall speak in your native tongue."

"Me too," Charles said.

"Thank you," Hok said. She, Fu, and Malao bowed.

"Please," Captain Rutger said. "Dispense with the formalities. We shall spend a small amount of time getting acquainted; then we will eat. After seeing the signal flags, I knew we were expecting friends. I am doubly pleased that it is you, Charles. I've taken the liberty of having my cook throw something together. I suppose you are famished."

Charles saw Fu's eyes light up.

"Thank you," Charles said. "We left in a hurry before sunrise and didn't pack any supplies besides water. We're starving."

"Come below, then," Captain Rutger said. "We shall set you up straightaway."

As they crossed the deck, Charles watched Hok, Fu, and Malao marvel over what they saw. There were innumerable sheets, stays, ratlines, and ropes running in every direction, connecting the schooner's three towering masts to rows of reefed sails. Weathered sailors lounged about, darning socks or smoking cigars, and caged chickens and rabbits darted within their on-deck enclosures under the watchful eye of the ship's goat, whose sole purpose was to provide milk each morning for the officers' tea.

How Charles missed seafaring life. It was like having an entire city squeezed into a space not much larger than an average house. It made him feel secure.

They climbed belowdecks and weaved their way through rows of hammocks filled with sleeping men. These men would make up the second watch, and Charles recognized a few of the bearded faces. He looked forward to catching up with them.

As they neared Captain Rutger's cabin, Charles detected the smell of bacon. His mouth began to water and his stomach growled. Fu turned to him with eager eyes and said, "Is that what I think it is?"

"Yes, it is," Charles replied happily. "I hope you don't mind bacon for dinner. Considering all those chickens on deck, we'll likely have fresh eggs, too. We typically eat this combination for breakfast, and it might seem a little odd."

Fu grinned. "Any man who serves breakfast food for dinner is a friend of mine!"

Captain Rutger laughed, and he led them into his private dining cabin, just aft of his living quarters. In the center of the room was a large table hanging from a series of ropes, designed to accommodate the ship's sway. Several benches were nailed to the floor around it. Fortunately, none of these precautions would be necessary while they were in the calm waters of the cove.

"This is neat!" Malao said, giving the swinging table a shove.

"So it is," Captain Rutger said. "Please, sit down and tell me what brings you here. I hope it wasn't to see Captain Henrik. He left this morning with most of our squadron to conduct some business in Taiwan."

Captain Rutger gave Hok a curious look as they all sat, and Charles thought he saw Hok blush.

"Why are you looking at me that way, sir?" Hok asked. "Do you know me?"

"I believe I do," Captain Rutger replied. "Your appearance is an interesting combination of two people I respect greatly. Namely, Captain Henrik and his strong, beautiful wife, Bing. You wouldn't happen to be OnYeen, would you?"

"I am," Hok replied. "Only, I am called 'Hok' now. These are my temple brothers, Fu and Malao. We are here because Charles thought you might give us refuge for a few nights. We have reason to believe that a general from the north known as Tonglong is looking for us."

"That sounds serious," Captain Rutger said.

"It is," Hok replied. "We don't intend to stay long, though. We've been discussing it, and we hope to find a way to get back to the north to join up with my mother and other members of a group that some call 'bandits' but others call 'the Resistance.' My brothers and I all have friends or family in the group, including another temple brother, a boy called Seh."

"I see," said Captain Rutger. "Charles did the right thing bringing you here. You will be safe. If you feel you can wait five or six days, so much the better. Your father will have returned by then, and I would bet my right arm that he will personally take you to your friends—that is, unless you would prefer to remain here with him for a while. The political climate is much more stable in this region, and I am certain your father would enjoy spending some time with all of you."

"We don't wish to inconvenience anyone," Hok said.

"Nonsense," Captain Rutger said. "Nothing would please me more. I have some knowledge of what the three of you have been through, including the destruction of your temple and your flight down the Grand Canal with that horrible creature Ying. I respect your courage, Hok."

"Ying isn't what he appears to be on the surface," Hok said in a cool tone. "How did you learn about these things?"

Captain Rutger raised his hands. "I am sorry if I've offended you. Our main source of intelligence concerning you and a host of other matters is a man called HukJee, a powerful black-market dealer in the northern city of Jinan. We intercept weapons shipments intended for a local warlord called HaiZhe here in the south and sell them to HukJee in the north. He pays us with information as often as he pays us with gold. We work almost exclusively with him, because we know he sells nearly all of his weapons to the Resistance. As you know, they oppose the Emperor's habit of living extravagantly while taxing the life out of China's poorest citizens. While we come from another land, we support their cause. And since we need to earn a living, this seems as honorable an occupation as any."

"Have you heard anything recently?" Charles asked.

"We've heard rumors that General Tonglong appears to be up to something big. So big that the Resistance feels they may need to shift their focus from the Emperor to Tonglong. They plan to keep an equally close eye on his mother, AnGangseh. They are a slippery pair."

A man came into the dining cabin carrying the largest platter of pork Charles had ever seen. Bacon, ham, pork chops, pickled pig's feet, and soused pig's face were piled precariously high. His mouth began to water, and across the table, he heard Fu's stomach grumble. Hok and Malao, however, looked like they were going to be sick.

"I think I'm going to step outside," Hok said.

"Me too," Malao muttered.

"Make sure you come back in time for the next course," Captain Rutger said. "I believe it is blood pudding!"

Hok looked at Malao, and Malao swallowed hard.

"Perhaps Malao and I will just turn in for the night," Hok said. "We've had a long day."

"As you wish," Captain Rutger said, standing. "I will take you to see my bosun. If you'd like something else to eat, just let him know. He will also clear a cabin for the four of you and sling your hammocks. I hope you don't mind bunking in the same room. It's a tight ship."

"Thank you, sir," Hok said. "We'll be fine."

Charles, Malao, and Fu echoed her thanks.

Captain Rutger stepped away from the table. "As much as I'd love to join you in this lovely meal, I should get back to my watch. Charles, I suggest you move your sloop to the far side of the island before you go to sleep tonight. I know it's a lot of work, but with all this talk of Tonglong, I would feel better knowing your ship was outside the cove. I feel a bit like a sitting duck here with the entire squadron out. I expect the seas to be calm for at least the next day, so you should have no trouble mooring her offshore. Have the fishing boat follow you to bring you back here."

"Aye, sir," Charles said between bites. "Fu and I can do it as soon as we finish eating."

Fu nodded his consent, grease dribbling down his chin.

"Excellent," Captain Rutger said, looking around the cabin. "Will you all be so kind as to join me here in the morning for breakfast? Say, an hour after sunrise?"

Charles and Fu nodded in enthusiastic agreement, their cheeks stuffed to the breaking point. Hok and Malao nodded politely, too.

"Very well," Captain Rutger said. "We shall meet again in the morning. Let us find a place for you to get some rest. With the current state of things, who knows what is going to happen next."

CHAPTER
18

AnGangseh sat in the back of the imperial sedan chair, stroking the Emperor's thinning hair. The gates of Shanghai were in sight. She leaned her perfect face over and purred in his ear, "Tell me, my dear, what is on the agenda for the next few days?"

The Emperor shifted in his seat and adjusted his brilliant yellow hat. "Fight club activities, of course. I have a few other things to attend to, but they are none of your concern."

AnGangseh ran a long fingernail along the side of his neck. "You know how much I enjoy witnessing great men in action, Your Highness. Won't you invite me to at least one of your meetings?"

"You shall see plenty of great men in action in the

pit arena," the Emperor replied, pushing her hand away. "Lei—Thunder—is to fight Golden Dragon. It is sure to be spectacular."

"Lei and Golden Dragon are but children. Will the warlords be there?"

"Of course. They wouldn't miss it for the world."

"Even Xie's father?" AnGangseh asked, glancing out the sedan-chair window at a giant of a man riding atop a surprisingly small horse. Xie, or Scorpion, was the Emperor's personal bodyguard. He glared at AnGangseh, a look of disgust on his face.

"Yes," the Emperor said. "The Western Warlord will be there, too. Though he rarely travels this far south or this far east, he recognizes what a great championship this will be. He will also be meeting with me and the other warlords. We shall have a splendid time, unless that uncouth Southern Warlord, HaiZhe, ruins it. He can be such a pest sometimes."

"Will you introduce me to them?" AnGangseh asked.

"I shall. You will join us in my private box during the bouts. Perhaps I will also allow you to attend one of our intimate postfight gatherings. Would you like that?"

AnGangseh looked deeply into the Emperor's eyes. "You have no idea how much that would please me."

"Then I shall make it so," he said, glancing away. "A meeting like that might change your life forever."

AnGangseh smirked. "I am counting on it."

Outside, Xie's horse whinnied loudly, and the sedan chair came to an abrupt halt.

"What is going on?" the Emperor demanded.

"It appears to be a messenger approaching, sir," Xie said. "He wears a soldier's uniform. Please remain inside until I determine whether or not he is a threat."

The sound of pounding hooves drew near, and AnGangseh pulled her wide black hood over her head. She leaned out the window and saw a man racing toward them on a horse. The horse was heaving, its sides thick with sweat and its mouth foaming.

Xie positioned himself well away from the sedan chair and hailed the rider. The rider slowed and finally stopped before Xie. He dug through a large bag attached to his saddle and handed two items to Xie. One was a small scroll. The other was a square wooden box with sides roughly the length of Xie's forearm. Xie shook the box, and the rider grimaced.

"Is there a problem?" Xie asked.

"No, sir," the rider replied.

"On your way, then," Xie said.

The rider left, and Xie headed for the sedan chair atop his horse. He handed the box and the scroll to the Emperor through an open window and retreated, muttering something under his breath.

AnGangseh looked at the items and grinned. The small scroll was obviously for her. Its wax seal contained the imprint of a cobra. As for the box, it had been quite ornate at one time, but now the tight-fitting seams were stained with dark brown blotches, and the fine hinges were corroded. On the lid was a clump of hardened wax imprinted with the image of a mantis.

"Do you recognize these seals?" the Emperor asked.

AnGangseh nodded. "The ssscroll is for me. I believe the box is for you."

"What's in it? It is surprisingly heavy."

"Good news, I think," AnGangseh said. "Aren't you going to open it?"

The Emperor looked at her hesitantly. "It smells awful."

"I'll do it, then," she said, taking the box. "Let me ask you a question first. How would you feel if you no longer had to deal with HaiZhe, the man you just referred to as 'uncouth' and a 'pest'?"

"I don't know. I suppose that would depend on who were to replace him."

"What about my ssson?"

The Emperor's eyebrows rose up. "Tonglong? I am sure he could easily find justification to unseat HaiZhe, but HaiZhe is far too cunning to ever let anyone get close enough to even talk with him, let alone demand that he step down."

"What if Tonglong was to eliminate him?"

"Tonglong eliminate HaiZhe and become the Southern Warlord?"

"Perhaps."

"What are you trying to say?"

"I am sssaying that Tonglong is very ambitious," AnGangseh said, "and he happens to be in the area. He is certainly up to sssomething. Anyone who wronged his father had better be wary. HaiZhe was on that list. Do you know about Tonglong's father?"

"I do," the Emperor said. "My family may be on that list, too. I have cousins in the south."

AnGangseh stroked the Emperor's arm. "Then you should keep your eyes open. I will do the sssame. If I notice anything sssuspicious, I promise I will notify you immediately. All I ask in return is that you remember me as the one who is looking out for you."

"I suppose I should never underestimate anyone," the Emperor said. "Least of all a former Fight Club Grand Champion like Tonglong. Just how far is he willing to go?"

AnGangseh tapped the side of the box and smiled. She pried the lid off with her sturdy fingernails and handed the box to the Emperor, her black eyes sparkling. "I believe *this* may answer your question."

The Emperor took the box and looked inside. As he came to realize what he was staring at, its nauseous odor striking him square in the face, he choked violently and hurled the box out the window.

AnGangseh caught a glimpse of HaiZhe's pale head as it tumbled from the box, and a smile slithered up the side of her deadly beautiful face.

Never underestimate anyone, indeed.

*K*A-BOOM! BOOM! BOOM! BOOM! BOOM!

Charles was shaken awake by the sound and concussion of cannons being fired from a ship's broadside. There could be no mistaking that unearthly sequence that rolled like thunder in the distance.

"All hands on deck!" roared Captain Rutger, and Charles heard feet pounding above and around him.

"What is happening?" Hok asked from across the dark cabin.

"We're under attack," Charles said, jumping to his feet and strapping his pistols across his bare chest. "You three stay down here. This is a gunfight. There is no place for kung fu up there."

Another sequence of *BOOMS!* echoed across the

cove, and the schooner's starboard side shook as three cannonballs found their mark, bouncing off the hull.

"They are still a ways off," Charles said. "If they get much closer, those balls will break through the ship's sides. Stay away from the walls."

Charles raced onto the deck and heard Captain Rutger's voice cry out in the crisp night air, "They've destroyed the batteries and are entering the cove! It's a Chinese man-o-war, and there are shapes in the sea beyond it. There is no telling how many ships they have out there. Clear the decks, men!"

Sailors began heaving overboard anything on deck that wasn't a weapon. Wooden chicken coops and rabbit pens soon littered the water, floating atop the waves. Through a wall of chicken feathers, Charles saw Malao poke his head out of a hatch, throw a rope around the neck of the ship's goat, and lead it belowdecks.

"Stay out of the way!" Charles shouted in Malao's direction as a gang of young powder boys raced toward the hatch. They dropped down with alarming speed, returning moments later with armloads of gunpowder, shot, and wadding for the cannons on deck.

"Starboard gun teams, to your stations!" Captain Rutger commanded, and men began to assemble in tight formations around the schooner's ten cannons on the ship's right side, facing their oncoming attacker. Tendrils of acrid smoke started to rise from buckets of slow match being lit next to each great gun.

"Incoming!" someone shouted from high atop the mainmast, and Charles heard a single enemy cannon erupt. Several sailors hit the deck, but Charles stood his ground defiantly. He stared toward the mouth of the cove and caught a glimpse of the approaching cannonball flying a few hands above the water. The ball dipped, skipped across the water, and went airborne again. It skipped two more times, its last short hop sending it harmlessly over the schooner's starboard stern rail. It rolled noisily over to port, stopping next to the helmsman's foot.

A powder boy scooped it up and tossed it over the side so that no one would trip over it.

"They're getting close!" Captain Rutger shouted. "Sharpshooters, to the tops!"

That was Charles' cue. He hurried to the nearest ratline and climbed aloft to a dizzying height with a speed and agility that would have made Malao proud. Once there, he hooked his legs and one elbow into the rigging and withdrew his pistols.

"Rig the splinter netting!" Captain Rutger ordered, and Charles looked down to watch netting fall from strategic locations among the lower shrouds. Sailors raced about, tying the nets up so that they formed a webbed ceiling above the deck. The netting was designed to catch any blocks or boom shards that might be blasted free from overhead by enemy fire.

"Prepare yourselves for battle, men!" Captain Rutger roared, and the gunners pulled large handkerchiefs from their pockets, tying them on their heads to keep hair and sweat out of their faces and away from the slow match.

Charles looked over at the enemy ship, nearer now, and he was certain that it was Tonglong's man-o-war. He called down, "On deck there! That ship belongs to General Tonglong! I'm sure of it."

"Aye, aye!" shouted Captain Rutger in response. "Thank you for the confirmation. Let us—"

KA-BOOM! BOOM! BOOM! BOOM! BOOM!

Cannons erupted in rapid sequence from Tonglong's ship, sending a hailstorm of iron and lead toward the schooner. A cannonball the size of Charles' head slammed into the ship's railing below, sending a shower of gigantic splinters in every direction. A sailor cried out and fell to the deck, an enormous splinter of oak protruding from the center of his chest.

"Somebody help that man!" Captain Rutger ordered. "Now it's our turn, mates! Remember, wait for the roll! On my mark . . ."

Charles felt the schooner dip slightly as a wave rolled beneath them. The ship began to rise again with the next swell, and as it reached the wave's crest, Captain Rutger cried, "FIRE!"

The schooner's starboard broadside erupted, its cannons disappearing in their own smoke. Thick haze drifted skyward, and Charles could taste the burnt air around him.

KA-BOOM! BOOM! BOOM! BOOM! BOOM!

Tonglong's ship fired another devastating sequence. How had they fired again so quickly? Charles wondered. They must have added more cannons since he had seen their ship a few weeks ago. No gun team could reload and fire a cannon that fast.

KA-BOOM! BOOM! BOOM! BOOM! BOOM!

Again, cannon fire erupted from Tonglong's vessel, and this time several of Captain Rutger's men fell, either dead or wounded. Tonglong must be using grapeshot now instead of cannonballs. If they switched to chain shot and aimed for the schooner's rigging, Charles would have to—

KA-BOOM! BOOM! BOOM! BOOM! BOOM!

Another round of cannon fire confirmed Charles' worst fear. All around him, spars and sailcloth began to tumble into the sea, ripped to shreds by long sections of chain that had iron balls welded to each end. Several of his sharpshooting compatriots were torn from the rigging without having fired a single shot. Tonglong's vessel was likely within pistol range by now, but the combined smoke from both ships' cannons left Charles nearly blind.

"On my mark . . . ," Captain Rutger bellowed from below. "FIRE!"

The roar of the schooner's cannons was answered by the roar of soldiers' voices aboard Tonglong's ship. They were not cries of agony but cries of war. Most of the schooner cannons must have missed their mark.

Charles felt a sudden powerful jolt as Tonglong's vessel slammed into Captain Rutger's moored schooner.

"Prepare to be boarded!" Captain Rutger shouted, and netting dropped from the ratlines, covering the sides of the ship like a curtain.

Charles peered down through the thick smoke and could just make out Chinese soldiers slashing through the schooner's boarding nets with wicked-looking broadswords. Other soldiers followed immediately behind with boarding axes, sinking them deep into the schooner's thick wooden hull to gain purchase before leaping over the schooner's starboard rail, onto the deck.

Charles took aim at a boarding soldier, then paused. His pistols were only single-shot devices, and he possessed just two. If he used them up now, he would never get off the ship. Loading would be impossible with all this activity. He slipped them back into the holsters across his chest and climbed down into the melee.

Soldiers and sailors were fighting everywhere in solo battles, members of both sides getting hung up on dangling ropes and broken spars or tripping over the bodies of their fallen comrades. The Dutch sailors had abandoned the cannons in favor of pistols and cutlasses, while the Chinese soldiers carried large broadswords and boarding axes, plus pistols of their own.

Charles backed up to the ship's far rail, away from the action, and realized that he was shaking. They were losing the battle, and still, the enemy came. They didn't appear to be highly skilled, but they were capable and there were so very many of them.

A sailor cried out from the topmast, and Charles looked up to see flames. A sharpshooter's musket blast must have ignited one of the canvas topsails. Sharpshooters all along the mizzen tops were shouting at one another, jumping down into the sea.

"Charles!" someone growled in Chinese. "Over here!"

Charles ran to the bow and found Fu hauling two
people out of the water, one in each hand. The first
was a small boy, and the second was an older man.
Charles stepped closer and realized that he knew the
man. It was LoBak. Perhaps the boy was ShaoShu.

"Fu, Malao, Hok!" Charles scolded. "You *must*
take cover. If you stay exposed like this, you're bound
to get—"

Malao suddenly shrieked and leaped clear over
Charles' head. Charles turned to see him land a perfect sidekick to the temple of a soldier wielding a
broadsword. The man dropped in a heap, and Malao
tossed the sword to Fu.

Malao turned to Charles. "You were saying?"

Charles opened his mouth to reply, but Captain
Rutger cried out, "Charles! Come, quick!"

Charles raced toward the captain's voice and found
him leaning against the schooner's starboard rail, a
wide stream of blood pouring from his scalp.

"Tell the men to abandon ship," Captain Rutger
gasped. "They won't want to do it, but they must pre-
serve themselves. I would tell them myself, but I don't
have the strength."

Charles looked about to see how best to begin the
evacuation, when he sensed someone staring at him.
He looked across to Tonglong's ship and saw a man
with a ridiculous number of pistols crisscrossing his
chest. The man pulled one from its holster and aimed
it at Charles.

Quick as a flash, Charles twisted away from Captain
Rutger and pulled out a pistol of his own. He raised

his arm in the man's direction and to his surprise heard the man's pistol discharge.

Charles felt nothing. He glanced down and verified that he was untouched. He looked over at Captain Rutger and saw a neat hole in the captain's forehead.

"No!" Charles cried, and he fired at the spot where the man had stood. But he was already gone.

Charles stood and began to shout at the top of his lungs in Dutch, "Captain Rutger is dead! He ordered us to abandon ship! Repeat! Captain Rutger is dead! Abandon ship!"

"Never!" came the cries from fore and aft. The sailors began to fight with increased vigor.

Charles threw his arms into the air in frustration. At a loss about what to do, he ran back over to his friends. Hok, LoBak, and the boy were in the middle of a heated discussion. Fu and Malao were keeping the soldiers at bay with a variety of weapons they'd picked up.

Charles loomed over the others and spoke in Chinese. "We have to abandon ship. What are you arguing about?"

Hok pointed to the boy. "This is ShaoShu. He and LoBak have escaped from the hold of Tonglong's warship. LoBak sees the value of running away, and we're trying to convince ShaoShu to come, too."

Charles looked up at the burning rigging, then at ShaoShu. "How much more convincing do you need? The ship is on fire!"

"Exactly," ShaoShu said. "It's sort of my fault. I

think I might be able to sneak back onto Tonglong's boat and get back into his commander's good graces. I could get information to Hok and you and everyone else about Tonglong's future plans."

Charles raised an eyebrow. "Good idea, but make up your mind, quick. My sloop is anchored on the opposite side of the island, and we must make a break for it."

Hok huffed. "If you insist on staying with Tonglong, ShaoShu, go with him to Shanghai. There is a big fight club event there in three days, and he is bound to attend. Seek out a fighter called Golden Dragon, and tell him who you are. Tell him about Tonglong and about us. He is our older temple brother. Let him know that we are headed back to the north. If he needs to find us, he should get a message to a woman named Yuen at the Jade Phoenix restaurant in the city of Kaifeng."

"But how is ShaoShu going to get back into anyone's good graces?" LoBak asked. "Tonglong hasn't questioned him yet about his possible acquaintance with me, but it's only a matter of time. He needs a convincing story."

Hok tore a silk thread from around her neck and handed it to ShaoShu. At the end of the thread dangled a tiny jade crane. "This might help," she said. "Give it to Tonglong and tell him LoBak was killed trying to flee this ship with a girl and a teenager with a face carved like a dragon. Do not admit that you know Ying, LoBak, or me. Ever."

ShaoShu nodded.

"Fair enough," LoBak said. "But what about our supposed remains? Tonglong will search this ship for bodies."

"Leave that to me," Charles said. "I'll have to sink this schooner just to get the crew to abandon it. Now, everyone, to the stern! There are lifeboats there. Climb into one and start rowing to shore. I'll catch up with you. ShaoShu, you stay here with me for the moment. Go!"

Hok grabbed LoBak by the arm and hurried away, with Malao and Fu leading the charge, weapons whirling.

Charles pointed over the side of the ship. "ShaoShu, Tonglong's boat is beginning to drift away. He knows he's won. You're going to have to swim for it."

"No problem," ShaoShu replied.

"Good luck, Little Mouse," Charles said, raising his remaining loaded pistol. "Swim for the bow. I'll watch your back."

ShaoShu nodded and gripped a small pouch near his waist, then dove headfirst into the black water, out of sight.

$\mathcal{S}$haoShu surfaced near the bow of Tonglong's warship. He treaded water until he was alongside the craft, then lifted his mouse's pouch out of the water.

The mouse began to squirm, and ShaoShu smiled. It had survived. He felt around the darkness until his hands happened upon a dangling section of rigging that had spilled overboard from high above. He tested its strength by yanking on it, and it held firm.

ShaoShu began to climb and didn't stop until he'd reached a dizzying height. He looked along the sails and saw no soldiers standing on the slats like he'd seen earlier. They had all climbed down to join the hand-to-hand combat.

ShaoShu glanced down at the deck and noticed

with interest that it was empty. Everyone must still be aboard the Round Eye's ship. He thought about climbing down when he detected movement below. It was Tonglong, coming out of his cabin. He was alone, heading for the stern.

Tonglong froze, and ShaoShu saw a small boatload of Round Eyes approaching through the smoky darkness. With all of Tonglong's men aboard their ship, these sailors were attempting a sneak attack.

The small boat thumped against the warship's stern, and a Round Eye reached up, taking hold of the much higher stern rail. He began to climb up the side of the ship, and Tonglong ran toward him. With a flash of silver, Tonglong unsheathed his straight sword and lopped off both of the man's hands. The Round Eye screamed and splashed into the water.

ShaoShu watched with wide eyes as a second Round Eye stood in the small boat, pointing a musket at Tonglong.

"Hey!" someone shouted from the deck, and ShaoShu saw Lei appear behind Tonglong with a pistol in each hand. He fired one, striking the Round Eye, and the man toppled out of the boat.

A third Round Eye stood, raising a pistol.

BANG!

Lei fired his second pistol, and this Round Eye fell backward into the small boat, his unfired pistol dropping into the water.

Oddly, Tonglong staggered wildly, and he, too, toppled over unconscious, onto the deck. Confused,

ShaoShu stared at him and saw that one of his cheeks and his ear on that side of his face were badly powder-burned. Also, the collar of his robe was on fire. Lei's second pistol had discharged right next to Tonglong's head, and the concussion had knocked him out while the blast had ignited his robe.

Lei dropped to his knees and patted Tonglong down, quickly extinguishing the flames. Then he did a curious thing. He looked around to make sure he was alone; then he snapped the cord Tonglong wore around his neck, slipping the special key into one of his holsters.

ShaoShu curled up as tightly as he could in the rigging, hoping Lei wouldn't see him, when he saw that there was one more Round Eye still in the small boat. The Round Eye pushed his fallen comrade off of himself, climbed over the rail, and leaped onto the deck, a long sword in one hand.

"Lei, look out!" ShaoShu cried.

Lei's expression changed to one of genuine sur-prise as he looked up to see the Round Eye charging toward him. Lei reached beneath his right pant leg, pulled out a small pistol, and fired.

The lead ball struck the Round Eye in the face, and he dropped to the deck.

Lei blew the smoke out of his pistol's short bar-rel and glared up at ShaoShu. He did not look happy. He pointed to the holster that held Tonglong's key, raised a finger to his lips as if to silence ShaoShu, then made a pretend pistol with his fingers, aiming it at ShaoShu and dropping his thumb like a pistol's hammer.

ShaoShu got the message.

As he was trying to decide whether he should climb down, ShaoShu was nearly thrown from the rigging by a violent *KAAA-BOOOOOOM!*

A huge explosion tore through the side of the Round Eye's ship, and a fountain of water rose high into the air. The schooner began to sink instantly. Charles must have rigged an explosion inside the boat's hold, below the waterline. Soldiers began to jump into the water and swim back to Tonglong's man-o-war, and Round Eye sailors swam toward shore. The suction created by the sinking ship pulled many beneath the waves, and some, mostly soldiers, never resurfaced. Before ShaoShu could count to one hundred, the schooner had vanished.

The surviving soldiers flooded onto the warship's deck and began to cheer and sing. Their victory was complete, and they hadn't even had to call in the soldiers on the merchant vessels still waiting outside the cove.

Tonglong regained consciousness amid the festivities, with Lei at his side and a large group of men staring down at him. He did not look pleased. ShaoShu was still in the rigging, but he came down the moment Lei pointed up at him.

Tonglong ordered Lei and ShaoShu into his private cabin, and he took a seat behind his writing desk.

"Start talking, ShaoShu," Tonglong said. "Last I

knew, Lei was questioning your loyalty and you were tied up in the hold. How did you escape?"

ShaoShu explained how his mouse had chewed through his ropes and how he untied LoBak when the battle began, because LoBak had said that they needed to go onto the deck in case the boat sank. ShaoShu then told how LoBak leaped overboard in the thick smoke of the warship's cannons to escape and how he chased after LoBak in order to report back to Lei what LoBak was up to. ShaoShu said that he saw LoBak climb onto the Round Eye's ship and begin talking with a girl and a teenager with a tattooed face when the three of them were killed by a wave of cannon blasts. ShaoShu finished the story by holding out the jade crane. "I climbed onto the Round Eye's boat to see if LoBak really was dead. I took this from the dead girl."

Tonglong didn't look convinced. He took the crane and stared at it intently. "Why did you bring me this?"

"I actually took it for myself, sir. I like it. It's shiny. But you can have it, if you want."

Tonglong's eyes narrowed. "Do you know the name Hok?"

"I know the word, sir. It's a bird. A crane, like the one in your hand."

"What about Ying?"

"Eagle, sir? I don't believe I've ever seen an eagle."

Tonglong shook his head. "What did the teenager's tattooed face look like?"

"Kind of like a dragon, sir. It was hard to see with all the smoke."

"Hmm," Tonglong said. "You didn't intentionally help LoBak escape, did you, ShaoShu?"

ShaoShu shook his head.

"With all due respect, sir," Lei said, "I would like to say that I no longer question ShaoShu's intentions. I know I had my suspicions, but he has recently proven himself to me. He saved my life and quite possibly yours, too."

"How so?" Tonglong asked.

"The Round Eyes who came over in the small boat—one of them nearly succeeded in taking my life with his sword, and being unconscious, you would surely have been next. ShaoShu warned me, giving me time to kill the foreigner."

Tonglong gently touched the side of his powder-burned face and glared at ShaoShu. He sat back with the jade crane and reached for the cord that he'd been wearing around his own neck. When his fingers came up empty, he leaped to his feet, shouting, "My necklace! My key! It's gone!" He slammed his fist on the desk and scowled at ShaoShu and Lei.

Lei lowered his eyes. "With the utmost respect, sir, I do not know why you are glaring at me. I am not the thief in this room. I don't even know what key you're talking about."

ShaoShu opened his mouth to object but quickly closed it again when he saw Lei discreetly form a pretend pistol behind his back and shoot him.

"Do you have something to say for yourself, Shao-Shu?" Tonglong snapped.

"I was just going to ask if you wanted me to go look for it on the deck, sir," ShaoShu said. "Maybe the flames that burned your collar also burned the cord that held the key."

Tonglong paused, considering something. "That is a good idea, ShaoShu. Lei, spread the word among the men that I have lost a key. Offer a reward, then make preparations to set sail. The fight club championship is in two and a half days, and it will take us two full days to get there with the damage we have sustained. You don't want to miss your big chance to win it all, do you?"

"No, sir!" Lei said. "I'll get right to it." He bowed and hurried out of the room.

Tonglong stared hard at ShaoShu, and ShaoShu did his best to hold Tonglong's gaze. *Never back down from a bully,* he thought.

Tonglong pursed his lips. "I believe you, ShaoShu. If *I* ever question your loyalty, I will not tie you up in the hold. I will kill you. You know that, don't you?"

"Yes, sir."

"Good." Tonglong rubbed the side of his powder-burned face again and glanced at the spot where Lei had stood.

"When we arrive in Shanghai, I may have another job for you."

CHAPTER 21

Two days later, ShaoShu stepped onto the docks of Shanghai's wharf with mixed emotions. He was happy that he was in Tonglong's good graces and glad that he'd been able to steer clear of Lei since the attack, but he was sad that he had been separated from his friends once again. Perhaps he would make a new friend today in Golden Dragon. Tonglong wanted him to run an errand at the Shanghai Fight Club, and he hoped to be able to sneak away for a few moments and find Hok's older temple brother.

ShaoShu walked calmly away from the ship, and once he was out of sight of the deck, he raced through Shanghai's crowded streets at a dead run, following the directions Tonglong had given him. He arrived at the fight club far sooner than anyone would have anticipated, and he planned to make the most of the extra time. His errand shouldn't take long at all—just to pick up some event posters—so every moment counted.

For years, ShaoShu had wanted to see inside a fight club, and after showing the guards at the front door a letter from Tonglong, he nearly squealed with delight when he stepped inside this one. It far exceeded his expectations.

The gigantic windowless space was perfectly round, with a floor that sloped steadily downward toward the circular pit arena at the room's very center. The fights wouldn't begin until that night, but already the club was alive with activity. Workers brushed final coats of fresh whitewash on the brilliant stone walls, and an army of carpenters swarmed the tiered seating levels, polishing the hundreds of tables and thousands of chairs until the shiny black lacquer was mirror smooth. Ornate tapestries hung from the ceiling rafters, and lanterns made of gold flickered from every direction on the walls. Of all the fight clubs in China, he had heard that Shanghai's was the most grand, and he believed it.

ShaoShu couldn't resist puffing out his chest and walking down one of the sloped aisles like an important person, traveling all the way to the edge of the pit arena. He leaned over the elaborate railing and peered down, and his already wide eyes nearly popped out of his head. It was far bigger and deeper than he'd imagined. The widest part of the circular pit was roughly fifty paces across, and the brick walls lining it stood higher than four men standing atop each other. The floor was made of compacted dirt, and there was a single large wooden door that Tonglong had told him led to a series of tunnels beneath the fight club. That door was the only way into or out of the pit, and those tunnels were his current destination.

ShaoShu looked around, trying to figure out how to access the tunnels without jumping down into the pit, when the pit entry door swung open and someone entered the pit arena. It was Golden Dragon. ShaoShu recognized him from the posters plastered up and down Shanghai's streets. He had short black hair and a kind face, and he looked much younger in person than he did in the posters. His body, however, looked like it belonged on someone else entirely. He was shirtless, and taut muscles rippled across his shoulders and chest. He was wearing standard-issue silk army pants like Tonglong's soldiers, but his thick thighs and calves threatened to burst the seams with every step he took.

A second person entered the pit arena and closed the door behind him. This man was several years older than Golden Dragon, and larger. Where Golden Dragon was lean solid muscle, this man was burly. His forearms were larger than ShaoShu's thighs.

Both Golden Dragon and the big man began to stretch as though warming up for exercise. ShaoShu was more flexible than anybody he had ever met, but Golden Dragon impressed him. He stood on one leg with his back straight and lifted his other leg high into the air with both knees locked. His legs were in a perfectly straight line, up and down, with one heel on the ground and the other heel pointed at the sky. That took not only flexibility, but also tremendous strength. ShaoShu couldn't even do it.

After some more impressive moves of flexibility and strength, Golden Dragon looked at the man and said, "Let's roll."

"Remember to take it easy on me," the big man replied. "We're just warming up for tonight."

Golden Dragon nodded, then bowed. The man returned the bow, and they began to grapple.

ShaoShu took a seat next to the pit arena railing. Even though he was in a hurry, he wouldn't miss this for the world.

Within moments, it became clear that Golden Dragon, while smaller, was far superior. His fluid style and lightning-quick moves continuously left his opponent grasping at nothing but shadows. Golden Dragon soon seemed to grow bored, and in the blink of an eye, he slipped behind his opponent, jumped onto the man's back, and wrapped his legs around his midsection. Then he slid his right arm around in front of the man's neck, grasped his own right wrist with his left hand, and leaned backward.

The man choked loudly as Golden Dragon's elbow aligned with his Adam's apple, and then Golden Dragon bent his arm so that his elbow moved away from the big man's throat. The big man stopped choking, but to ShaoShu's surprise, his face turned bright red and then purple, and an instant later, his eyes rolled back into his head and his body went limp.

Golden Dragon quickly dropped to his feet, supporting the much larger man and gently laying his opponent down on the pit arena floor. He checked the man's pulse.

ShaoShu stood and began to clap. "That was great! Is he dead?"

Golden Dragon looked up at him. "No, he's not dead. He's unconscious. Who are you?"

ShaoShu glanced around to make sure none of the workers were close. He leaned over the pit arena railing and said in a low whisper, "My name is ShaoShu, and I am friends with Hok, Fu, and Malao. I have a message for you."

Golden Dragon's eyebrows rose up. He scanned the fight club, too. "Come down here so we can talk."

"Me? How?"

"Jump."

"What?"

"Just jump," Golden Dragon said in an impatient tone. "I'll catch you. Try to lie down in the air as you fall."

ShaoShu looked around again and caught one of the workers staring at him. Before anyone could stop him, he swung his legs over the railing and launched himself toward Golden Dragon as though he were flopping onto a bed on his back.

Golden Dragon caught him with ease, setting him onto his feet.

"Well done," Golden Dragon said.

"Thanks," ShaoShu replied. He nodded toward the unconscious man, still lying on the pit arena floor. "Is it safe to talk here?"

"Safer than most places in this building. There are guards everywhere, but none of them would dare come into the pit with me. Don't worry about my friend here, either. It will be a while before he regains consciousness."

ShaoShu grinned. He liked Golden Dragon.

"What is this message you're talking about?" Golden Dragon asked.

"Well, first of all, Hok told me to tell you that—"

Golden Dragon's body suddenly went rigid, and he held up a callused hand.

"What is it?" ShaoShu whispered.

"Shhh," Golden Dragon said. "Someone is coming. Someone bad. Keep quiet, and let me do the talking."

ShaoShu listened and soon heard footsteps on the opposite side of the pit arena door. A huge brown face filled a little window in the door, and the door swung inward, into the tunnel. A petite woman wearing a large black silk hood glided into the pit. The gigantic man whose big brown face had been in the window remained in the doorway, his massive arms folded.

Golden Dragon bowed, and the woman asked, "Who are you?"

When Golden Dragon didn't answer, ShaoShu realized that she was talking to him. He was about to reply when Golden Dragon spoke first. "He is my ring boy."

"Your what?"

"My ring boy," Golden Dragon said. "He is responsible for assisting me tonight. He will carry my water, my towels, my—"

"Look at me, child," the woman interrupted. She stepped closer to ShaoShu and pushed back her hood to reveal a beautiful face and long, luxurious hair. Her black eyes shone bright, and she stared deeply into ShaoShu's eyes.

ShaoShu suddenly felt light-headed, and the room began to spin. He tried to look away, but for some reason he could not unlock his eyes from hers.

"Do you know who I am?" the woman asked.

ShaoShu shook his head.

"I am AnGangseh. General Tonglong, the new Sssouthern Warlord, is my ssson. I believe you know him."

ShaoShu nodded.

"What are you doing here?"

ShaoShu felt himself beginning to answer, even though he didn't want to. Words started to form in his mouth, and Golden Dragon slapped him on the back, bringing him back to his senses. He looked away, shaking his head to clear it.

"I asked what you are doing here," AnGangseh repeated.

"Your question was already answered, gracious lady," Golden Dragon said. "He is helping me. If you'll pardon us, we have work to do before tonight's event."

"You will answer my questions until I am sssatisfied!" AnGangseh hissed, turning to the huge man in the doorway. "Isn't that right?"

The big man nodded.

ShaoShu cleared his throat. "My name is ShaoShu, miss. I work for your son. I came here to pick up some posters for tonight's event, and I met Golden Dragon. He asked me to help him."

AnGangseh flicked a piece of white hair from the hem of her black robe. "Golden Dragon's opponent tonight is a young man called Lei, who is now my ssson's commander in this region. I find it odd that you work for Tonglong, but you are going to help Golden Dragon."

"If Lei had asked me to help him, I would have. But he didn't. Golden Dragon did. I had to say yes. This is the most exciting thing to ever happen to me!"

"Leave the kid alone," said the huge man in the doorway. "He's answered your questions. We have more important things to do."

AnGangseh turned toward the man. "You will provide your opinion only when it's asked for, Xie. I have reason to be sssuspicious of Golden Dragon and anyone connected with him." She looked back at Golden Dragon. "Tell me about Cangzhen Temple."

"I don't know what you're talking about," Golden Dragon replied.

"I think you do," AnGangseh said. "I believe your real name is Long and that you are a fugitive. All Cangzhen monks have been deemed enemies of the ssstate. What do you have to sssay to that?"

"Nothing," Golden Dragon said.

"Of course not," AnGangseh snapped. "Let me leave you with this bit of information, then. My ssson has your precious dragon ssscrolls. He no longer has use for them, ssso I am going to burn them. Better yet, maybe I'll ssslice them into little sheets for Tonglong's sssoldiers to use in the latrine."

Golden Dragon's jaw tightened noticeably, and AnGangseh laughed.

"I knew it!" she said. "You *are* Long! Wait until I tell Tonglong."

Xie took a step into the pit arena, glaring at Golden Dragon, daring him with his eyes to make a move.

"Never mind, Xie," AnGangseh said. "After tonight, it won't matter. Lei is going to kill him. Make sure he doesn't leave the fight club."

"I am not going anywhere," Golden Dragon said. "And I resent your accusations. We can discuss this further after tonight's bout. Right now, I need to complete my preparations. ShaoShu, come with me."

Golden Dragon walked past AnGangseh and Xie with his head held high, and ShaoShu followed him into the tunnels. After several twists and turns through the torch-lit corridors, they reached a room containing stacks of event posters.

"This is what you've come for," Golden Dragon said. "Now is not a good time to talk. Take your posters back to Tonglong and return here in two hours. Tell the guards you are my ring boy. They will be expecting you. Meet me near the pit arena again, and I'll take you someplace private so that you can tell me about Hok and the others. After that, I will tell you what you need to do to help me tonight."

"I'll do my best to return tonight," ShaoShu said, "but Tonglong might not let me do it. I am sorry things turned out this way for you."

"No need to be sorry. People were bound to find out eventually. I'll just have to think carefully about how I am going to handle things after I win."

"You really think you're going to beat Lei?"

"I don't have a choice, do I?"

"I guess not. Is there anything I can do?"

Golden Dragon shook his head. "I've gotten this far alone. I'll finish it alone. Maybe afterward I'll join up with Hok and the others. I had other plans, but they're of no use now." He looked around and pointed farther down the tunnel. "To exit, walk in that direction until you come to a fork. Keep to the right, and you will soon find a door that leads outside. Hopefully, I will see you in two hours." He gave ShaoShu a slight bow and walked off.

ShaoShu grabbed an armload of posters and left, following Golden Dragon's directions. He hurried back to Tonglong's ship and found Tonglong alone in his cabin.

"You're back at last," Tonglong said from behind his writing desk. "I was beginning to worry about you."

"I met Golden Dragon!" ShaoShu said excitedly, placing the posters in a neat stack on the floor. "He asked me to be his ring boy tonight! Can I do it, sir? Please?"

Tonglong folded his hands upon his desk. "How do you think Lei will feel about it?"

ShaoShu kicked at a ball of cat hair that drifted past. He shrugged.

"You don't like him very much, do you?"

ShaoShu shook his head.

"Why not?"

ShaoShu considered saying that Lei was a liar and a thief and that he was the one who stole Tonglong's key. However, he decided not to. Tonglong might not believe him, and then Lei would surely kill him. Instead, ShaoShu lowered his voice and said, "He scares me, sir."

"No need to worry about him right now," Tonglong replied. "He's at the fight club, preparing for tonight's bout. How is it that Golden Dragon asked for your assistance?"

ShaoShu's eyes brightened. "It just sort of happened, sir. We were talking, and then your mother came by, and—"

"My mother?" Tonglong interrupted. "Are you sure?"

"Yes, sir. She knew that I knew you."

Tonglong's eyebrows rose up. "I don't believe I've mentioned you in any of my communications, and I certainly haven't seen her yet in Shanghai."

"Maybe she just assumed I knew of you because you are famous, sir."

"I doubt it," Tonglong said, rubbing the powder burn on the side of his face. "She has been exchanging information with someone. Remember the other day I told you that I might have a job for you in Shanghai?"

"Yes, sir."

Tonglong pulled a small pistol from the folds of his robe. "When you return to the fight club, I would like you to switch this with the pistol Lei carries beneath his pant leg."

"Huh?"

"No questions," Tonglong said. "Figure out a way to do it before he enters the pit arena tonight."

ShaoShu turned the pistol over in his hands. It looked normal to him, but he doubted it was. He noticed Tonglong absentmindedly feeling for the necklace he no longer wore. "This is about your key, isn't it, sir?"

Tonglong lowered his hand. "No questions."

ShaoShu nodded. "I understand."

"Do you?"

ShaoShu thought for a moment. "Maybe not, but if this *is* about your key, you picked the right person."

"I know I did," Tonglong said, watching the ball of cat hair glide across the floor. "I always pick the right person. Now go do as you're told."

CHAPTER 22

AnGangseh sat in the back corner of Lei's fight club preparation room, nearly invisible with her black hood pulled over her head. Xie had returned to the Emperor, and she had very little time before she would be expected to return, too. Lei had better be on time.

Moments later, Lei rushed into the room and closed the door. He looked around, and AnGangseh stepped out of the shadows.

"Do you have it?" she asked.

"Yes," Lei replied. "Do you have the money?"

"Of course." AnGangseh set a bag on the floor and took a step back. "Go on, look."

Lei walked toward the bag and reached for it, then hesitated.

"It's not full of sssnakes, if that's what you're worried about," AnGangseh said. "Out of respect for your family, I wouldn't do that. Your father was a famous sssellout. He helped me many times." She smirked.

"Like father, like son," Lei said with a chuckle. He opened the bag and removed a *tael* of silver. "This has the Emperor's personal seal!"

"Of course. Where else would I have been able to obtain the amount we agreed upon? Just melt them down into sssilver bars, and no one will know where it came from. Now give me what's mine."

Lei reached into one of the holsters across his chest and removed Tonglong's key, admiring the entwined dragons that wrapped over and around the key's unique teeth. He tossed it to AnGangseh.

AnGangseh caught it and retied the dangling cord around her neck, then slipped the ornate key into the folds of her robe.

"I've never seen a key like that before," Lei said. "What is it for?"

"You wouldn't believe me if I told you," AnGangseh replied.

"You got it from HaiZhe, didn't you?"

"I received it before you were even born. How it came into my possession is none of your business."

"Well, you never thanked me for killing him, you know. That is one loose end you won't have to tie up."

"Thank you," AnGangseh said in a sarcastic tone.

"What are you going to do with the key?"

AnGangseh paused, considering her reply. "You are ssstill on my payroll, yes?"

"Yes," Lei said. "And as long as you keep paying me as well as you have been, I will continue to do your bidding, even after I win the fight club championship and climb higher up the Emperor's ranks."

AnGangseh nodded. "I was going to give the key to my sssecond husband, Mong, but he was not interested in ultimate power. He would rather lead a group of misfit bandits and their ssso-called 'Resistance' and waste time with our ssson, Ssseh. Instead, I entrusted whereabouts of the key to my firstborn, Tonglong. However, once you informed me that he had retrieved it, I began to have regrets. You could sssay that it is the key to the Forbidden City, and being the Emperor's mother no longer appeals to me. I would rather keep the key for myself and use it to become the current Emperor's wife."

"Well, good luck with that," Lei said. "I look forward to my next payment. You should leave now. I have to start preparing for my fight."

"It is sssuch a pleasure working with sssomeone as shallow as you," AnGangseh hissed, and she slipped out of the room.

CHAPTER 23

"**A**re you ready?" ShaoShu asked.

"I am always ready," Golden Dragon replied. "Let's go."

ShaoShu followed Golden Dragon through a maze of fight club tunnels on their way to the pit arena for the championship fight. Golden Dragon now knew everything ShaoShu knew, and Golden Dragon seemed more determined than ever to be victorious tonight.

As they walked, ShaoShu thought about Lei's numerous pistols. He had tried to tell Golden Dragon about his assignment to switch one of them for the pistol he had hidden in the folds of his robe, but Golden Dragon did not want to hear about it. He had said that he would not win by cheating. ShaoShu didn't exactly consider what he was supposed to do cheating, considering the ridiculous number of other pistols Lei would be carrying, but Golden Dragon would not listen.

As they neared the pit arena entrance, ShaoShu heard the arena announcer keeping the crowd excited.

"Ladies and gentlemen! We hope you've been enjoying yourselves tonight at the world-famous Shanghai Fight Club! So far this evening, you've seen amazing feats of courage and extraordinary exhibitions of will—but you have not seen anything yet. Finally, the event you've all been waiting for, the highly anticipated Fight Club Grand Championship! This bout will feature . . ."

ShaoShu tried his best to ignore it.

They arrived at the pit arena entrance and were stopped by a powerful-looking guard. The guard nodded respectfully to Golden Dragon and said, "Present your weapons, please."

Golden Dragon held up his hands.

"Very funny. Where are you hiding them?"

"I'm not hiding anything," Golden Dragon said. He spread his robe wide to expose nothing but skin and untied his sash to show that its underside did not contain any secret compartments.

"Look," the guard said. "It doesn't matter what weapons you bring, Golden Dragon. Nothing is off-limits in there. I just need to know what you have for crowd-security reasons. You can't expect me to believe that you are going to fight Lei, of all people, using only your bare hands."

"I can't control what you believe and what you don't believe," Golden Dragon said, "but I am only going to use my bare hands. Probably my arms, legs, and feet, too. No weapons."

"It's your funeral, then," the guard said. "I'll give you a moment to say goodbye to your ring boy. If you need anything, just let me know." He walked far down the tunnel and leaned against the wall.

"What should I tell Hok?" ShaoShu asked with a sigh.

"Hok?" Golden Dragon said. "You sound like you are saying goodbye. Do not worry so. Whatever will be, will be."

"How can you be so calm at a time like this?"

"Why shouldn't I be calm?"

"Because you're going bare-handed into a fight with a man who will be carrying six or seven loaded pistols, that's why!"

"Is that all?" Golden Dragon said. "I was told he carried more."

"You're crazy."

Golden Dragon smiled. "Perhaps you are the one who is crazy. You should learn to relax your mind. Focus your worries away. Chase a shadow sometime."

"Chase a shadow?"

"Take a chance on the unknown. My Dragon-style kung fu *sifu* used to call it 'chasing the shadow.' "

"I will try to remember that."

"Good," Golden Dragon said with a bow. "Now, I believe it is time."

ShaoShu returned the bow and watched as the guard walked back over to them. He bowed to Golden Dragon and opened the door as the announcer cried, *"Here he is, ladies and gentlemen, Golden DRAGON!"*

Golden Dragon entered the pit arena to enthusiastic applause. He bowed to the crowd, and ShaoShu heard someone behind him down the tunnel shout, "Enjoy this moment, Dragon, for it will be your last!"

ShaoShu turned to see Lei approaching, and he suddenly remembered what he still needed to do. As the guard began to close the pit arena door, ShaoShu said, "Wait, sir! Let me have just one more look."

"Hurry up," the guard grumbled.

ShaoShu poked his head into the pit arena and quickly snatched a handful of dirt from the ground. He took one last look at Golden Dragon, then pulled his head back inside the tunnel. The guard closed the door, and ShaoShu shoved his dirt-filled hand between his sash and his robe, next to the mouse's pouch.

"Fancy seeing you here," Lei said.

ShaoShu turned around, and Lei stepped up to him.

"I'm sorry," ShaoShu replied nervously. "I would have helped you if you asked."

Lei raised his hand as if to hit ShaoShu, but the guard intervened.

"Lei," the guard said. "You're about to go on. I need to see what you're packing tonight."

Lei scoffed and pulled open his robe to reveal six loaded pistols in their holsters across his chest.

"Anything else?" the guard asked.

"No," Lei replied.

ShaoShu's eyes widened. Was Lei lying? There was only one way to find out.

As Lei began to pull the folds of his robe back over his pistols, ShaoShu bent down and pulled his hand out of his sash. He shoved his face into his dirt-filled palm and inhaled deeply, unleashing a violent dirty sneeze all over the lower portion of Lei's right pant leg.

Lei recoiled in disgust, but ShaoShu had already taken hold of Lei's pant cuff and begun to wipe the snot from it. Lei stumbled, and as he attempted to right himself, ShaoShu leaned forward to block his view. He grabbed Tonglong's pistol from the folds of his robe and made the switch. Lei had indeed been lying.

By the time Lei regained his balance, ShaoShu was back to wiping snot. Lei and the guard were none the wiser.

Lei kicked ShaoShu in the ribs, and ShaoShu whimpered loudly. He rolled away, acting far more injured than he actually was. He knew the more distractions Lei had, the better.

Lei began to curse at him, and the guard said, "You're up, Lei." The guard opened the pit arena door, and ShaoShu heard the announcer say, *Everyone . . . let's make some noise for THUNDER!*"

The crowd yelled even louder for Lei than they had for Golden Dragon. Lei entered the pit arena and flashed his guns to the crowd. Their roar grew deafening.

The guard shut the door and shook his head, rubbing his ears. "I hate when he does that. It gives me a headache every time."

The guard turned his face to the small barred window in the pit arena door.

ShaoShu looked around and realized that that window offered the only view into the pit arena. There was no way he could wait through the entire match without seeing at least some of it. What if Golden Dragon needed his help? Wasn't that part of a ring boy's job?

"Excuse me," ShaoShu said to the guard. "May I take a look?"

"No."

"Why not?"

"Because I said so."

"But I am Golden Dragon's ring boy. I need to watch to see if he needs anything."

The guard chuckled. "He won't be needing anything where he's going."

ShaoShu pouted. "Will you help him if something bad happens?"

"Nope. Not my job."

"Whose job is it?"

"Don't know, don't care. Now be quiet. The fight is about to start."

ShaoShu had had enough. He was worried for Golden Dragon. Without giving it any more thought, he leaped onto the guard's back, wrapping his legs around the man's midsection like he'd seen Golden Dragon do.

"What the—" the guard began to say, but his words were cut short by ShaoShu's right arm digging into his throat. ShaoShu grabbed his own right wrist with his left hand and leaned back hard.

Unfortunately, for some reason the big man didn't go down. Instead, he thrashed and swung his arms wildly at ShaoShu, and ShaoShu thought he was going to get his head knocked off. He shifted his arms several different ways, but that merely made the guard more angry. ShaoShu gave the big man's neck one last squeeze, and the guard twisted around, trying to buck ShaoShu from his back. In the process, the guard tripped over his own feet and fell flat on his face, his left temple striking the stone floor with tremendous force. The man went limp.

ShaoShu climbed off the big man's back and looked down. The guard was still breathing, and a lump was quickly forming on his head, but he wasn't bleeding. He would be fine.

ShaoShu swiped the guard's ring of keys, shoved them in a pouch next to his mouse, and climbed onto the man's chubby behind. Standing there on his tiptoes, he found that he could just see through the barred window into the pit arena.

A gong sounded, and the fight began.

CHAPTER 24

The fight started with Golden Dragon and Lei circling one another, sizing each other up. This went on for some time, and ShaoShu began to grow anxious.

He glanced into the crowd and saw the Emperor's box directly across from him at the very edge of the pit arena. In the box sat the Emperor dressed in yellow, with AnGangseh at his side. On the Emperor's other side was Xie, and next to Xie was a very large man who was the spitting image of Xie, only older. ShaoShu had once heard Tonglong and Lei saying that the Emperor's bodyguard was the son of the Western Warlord, so ShaoShu guessed that's who the man was. On AnGangseh's other side sat Tonglong, now the Southern Warlord, and next to him was a frail-looking man. ShaoShu guessed that he was the Eastern Warlord.

Some of the crowd members began to boo the lack of action in the pit arena, and ShaoShu looked over to see Lei flash his guns again. The crowd began to chant:

"THUN-DER! THUN-DER! THUN-DER!"

Lei set his jaw and pulled out a pistol. Without warning, he fired a shot at Golden Dragon.

BANG!

ShaoShu saw the whole thing as if in slow motion, and he could hardly believe his eyes. Lei pulled the trigger, and in the momentary pause between the spark of the flint, the powder igniting, and the lead ball blasting forward, Golden Dragon dropped flat to the ground and the lead ball passed harmlessly over him.

The crowd went wild.

Without missing a beat, Golden Dragon leaped to his feet and sprang at Lei as he pulled out a second pistol. Golden Dragon grabbed the pistol with both hands, wrenching it out of Lei's grasp, and fired it into the compacted dirt floor.

BANG!

Golden Dragon threw the spent pistol down and in the blink of an eye managed to snatch a third pistol from one of Lei's holsters before Lei could back away.

The crowd cheered madly.

Golden Dragon began to stalk Lei with the unfired pistol in his hand, but Lei did nothing but retreat. The crowd began to heckle and taunt Lei for running away. They wanted to see him stand and fight.

"Let's do this like real men," Golden Dragon hissed.

BANG!

Golden Dragon fired the third pistol into the floor and threw it down.

"Real men! Real men!" someone shouted, and the crowd started chanting:

"GOL-DEN! DRA-GON! GOL-DEN! DRA-GON!"

ShaoShu saw Lei's face harden. He spat and pulled two pistols from the folds of his robe, holding one in each hand.

Golden Dragon edged toward Lei, who fired a quick shot with his right-hand pistol.

BANG!

Golden Dragon spun to his own right side, dodging the lead ball. However, in the same instant, Lei fired his left-hand pistol.

BANG!

This shot struck Golden Dragon in the upper portion of his left arm. He cried out in pain, and the crowd fell silent.

Ignoring his wound, Golden Dragon rushed across the pit to Lei, fast as lightning. He pinned Lei's arms to his sides in a powerful chest-to-chest bear hug. Lei hadn't even had time to retrieve another pistol.

The crowd roared with approval.

ShaoShu watched as Lei dropped his spent pistols and let his legs fall out from under him, pulling Golden

Dragon down with his dead weight. Golden Dragon compensated by arching his back and heaving Lei upright again, but the damage was done.

Lei had managed to retrieve the hidden pistol from under his right pant leg with his right hand and grab something else with his left hand from beneath his left pant leg. Lei's left wrist flicked forward along Golden Dragon's right thigh, and Golden Dragon howled, releasing his hold on Lei.

Golden Dragon took several steps back, and ShaoShu saw a long line of red running down Golden Dragon's leg. He looked over at Lei and saw that he was holding a knife in his left hand. The pistol was still in Lei's right hand, down by his waist.

The crowd turned deathly silent.

Golden Dragon glared at Lei, then rushed forward again.

"NO!" ShaoShu shouted. But it was too late. He watched in horror as Lei fired the pistol from his hip.

KA-BOOM!

The pistol exploded in Lei's hand with an immense blast of flames and smoke and a terrific thunder that echoed throughout the fight club.

Eager shouts of "What happened? What happened?" began to rain down from the crowd.

As the smoke cleared, ShaoShu saw Golden Dragon standing over Lei. Most of Lei's right side was gone. He was undoubtedly dead.

The crowd erupted into a frenzy. They began chanting again:

"GOL-DEN! DRA-GON! GOL-DEN! DRA-GON!"
ShaoShu looked up at the Emperor's seating area and saw that Xie was no longer there. The other members of the party were already filing out into a special tunnel entrance as the crowd danced and cheered around them.

Golden Dragon began to limp toward the pit entry door, and ShaoShu threw it open. He helped Golden Dragon through it, then closed it again, the crowd still chanting:

"GOL-DEN! DRA-GON! GOL-DEN! DRA-GON!"

"Are you okay, Golden Dragon?" ShaoShu asked.

"I'm fine," Golden Dragon replied. "But from now on, please call me Long."

"Whatever you say, Long. That was incredible!"

"Thanks," Long said, gripping his bloody right thigh with one hand and his upper left arm with the other hand. "What happened to the guard?"

"He tripped and hit his head," ShaoShu said, looking at Long's wounds. "Those really look like they hurt. Is there anything I can do?"

"You can help me out of here. I think—"

"HALT!" said a deep voice from down the tunnel. "Nobody is going anywhere."

ShaoShu frowned. It was Xie.

"Golden Dragon, you are under arrest," Xie said as he approached. "ShaoShu, you are under arrest, too, until it is determined whether or not you've committed any crimes by assisting this enemy of the state."

"Oh, no!" ShaoShu said.

"It's okay," Long said. "I expected as much." He grunted, clamping his hands down tighter.

"This way," Xie said, giving ShaoShu a shove. Xie directed them down a series of short tunnels before stopping outside a large prison cell with iron bars across the front. "Inside."

ShaoShu helped Long hobble into the cell, and Xie slammed the rusty door shut before walking away.

"Hey!" ShaoShu said. "What about his leg and arm?"

"I'm a soldier, not a physician," Xie said without breaking stride. He turned a corner and was gone.

ShaoShu looked at Long. "I want to help you."

"I'll be all right," Long said. He took off his robe and tore a long strip of silk free, wrapping it tightly around his wounded leg.

Long began tearing a second strip for his arm when they heard Xie shouting. ShaoShu listened intently, but with the echoing within the stone tunnels, he couldn't make out what Xie was saying.

Long looked at the prison cell bars. "You're pretty small. Do you think you could squeeze between them?"

"Gosh," ShaoShu said. "I almost forgot." He reached into a pouch attached to his sash and pulled out the ring of keys. "No need to squeeze if you have the keys! I tried your choke trick on the guard, but it didn't work. I got lucky. He knocked himself out against the ground."

Long laughed.

Xie began to shout even louder, and ShaoShu jumped to his feet. He tried several keys until he found the right one, then threw the key ring to Long. "I don't want them to jingle while I'm sneaking around."

Long nodded and tucked the keys behind his sash.

"I'll be right back," ShaoShu said, and hurried toward Xie's angry cries. After rounding a few corners, he caught sight of the big man smashing his huge fists against a heavy wooden door very much like the one leading to the pit arena. It even had a small barred window.

Xie stopped pounding and stuck his face against the window. "Let me in, Tonglong! Open this door and I may forgive you. Leave it closed and you're a dead man."

There was no response from the other side of the door, and Xie began to pound on it again. Brick dust billowed from the hinges, and ShaoShu saw a small hole open up next to the door's lowest hinge. As he stared at it, the pounding stopped.

"How did you get out?" Xie growled.

ShaoShu looked up at Xie and shrugged. "What is happening in there?"

"None of your business."

Xie went back to pounding on the door, and the small hole next to the hinge grew larger. Xie flew into a rage and began to shout again, focusing intently on the window.

ShaoShu couldn't contain his curiosity any longer.

He raced over to the hole and peered through with one eye, trying his best to keep his other eye focused on Xie.

Through the hole, ShaoShu saw a large meeting room. Ornate couches lined the walls, and thick carpet covered the floor. In the center of the room, Tonglong stood debating with the Emperor, the Eastern Warlord, the Western Warlord, and AnGangseh. Tonglong was wearing the white jade armor, and at his feet lay the white jade swords. The Emperor looked terrified.

ShaoShu stepped back from the hole and looked at the door. There was a handle but no lock. *The door must lock from the other side,* he thought. He examined the small hole and said, "If you are willing to help me, I think I can help you."

Xie stopped pounding and scowled at ShaoShu. "What could you possibly do for me?"

"I think I can squeeze through that hole and open the door from the other side."

Xie's eyes narrowed. "Why would you do that?"

"Because I don't trust Tonglong, and your boss looks scared."

"The Emperor isn't the only one I'm concerned about," Xie said. "The Western Warlord is my father. Something is very wrong. What do *you* want?"

"I want you to help me and Golden Dragon. We're not criminals, you know."

Xie nodded. "I'm beginning to believe that. Tonglong and his two-faced mother are the problem. We have a deal, little one. Help me get the Emperor and my father out of there, and I'll ask the Emperor to give you and Golden Dragon a pardon."

"I'll try my best," ShaoShu said. "Wish me luck." He bent down and stared at the hole again. Visions of Tonglong's father's final resting place began to run through his mind. He took a deep breath, exhaled, and pushed his head through the hole. It fit. As he began to wriggle his shoulders through, Tonglong raised his voice.

"Eastern Warlord," Tonglong said, picking up one of the jade swords, "I hereby request that our armies unite."

The Eastern Warlord put his hands out hesitantly, then pulled them back. "I need to think about this."

The Western Warlord sneered. "I don't need to think anymore. I am leaving." He turned away from the group, and Tonglong grabbed him by the collar, spinning him back around.

"Take your filthy hands off me!" the Western Warlord shouted, and he reached for the sword tucked into his sash.

ShaoShu popped his upper body through the hole and watched in disbelief as Tonglong dropped the jade sword, slipped his own sword from its sheath with deadly speed, and ran the blade through the Western Warlord's heart.

"NO!" cried Xie from the other side of the door.

ShaoShu pushed himself the rest of the way through and jumped to his feet. He turned the door handle, and to his relief, the lock disengaged. He gave the door a shove, and it swung open.

Xie roared, taking a step into the room, and Shao-Shu dove behind a large vase resting on the floor.

Tonglong pivoted toward the doorway, and ShaoShu saw him pull a pistol from the folds of his robe.

BANG!

The pistol fired, and Xie crashed to the floor. He lay still.

ShaoShu shuddered. He peered around the vase and saw Tonglong drop the pistol and pull a second one from his robe. He aimed it at the Eastern Warlord and asked, "Have you finished thinking yet?"

The Eastern Warlord dropped to his knees and kowtowed at Tonglong's feet. "I am your vassal."

"I thought you might be," Tonglong said. "You may rise and take one of the jade swords."

The Eastern Warlord stood and picked one up, and Tonglong pointed the pistol at the Emperor.

AnGangseh, who had been holding on to the Emperor's arm, released it and took a step backward. She smiled at Tonglong.

"Well, Mother," Tonglong said, "as the Round Eyes say, I believe it is time to pay the piper. I promised long ago to seek revenge against those who have betrayed my family, did I not?"

"You most certainly did," AnGangseh said.

Tonglong glared at the Emperor. "Say goodbye, traitor."

Tonglong pulled the trigger, and at the very last instant, ShaoShu saw him jerk his arm sideways.

BANG!

The pistol fired, its lead ball tearing through AnGangseh's throat. ShaoShu nearly cried out as she clawed at her neck and dropped to her knees, blood pouring between her fingers and over her long nails. She gurgled and hissed and somehow managed to form a solitary word.

"Why?"

Tonglong pointed to a single white cat hair clinging to the side of her black hood. "That's why."

AnGangseh hissed again and swiped at Tonglong, but he casually stepped out of the way. She swiped a second time, hitting nothing, then toppled over in a sea of her own blood. A moment later, she was gone.

ShaoShu watched Tonglong walk over to AnGangseh and tear a silk cord from around her neck. Dangling from the cord was a key entwined with dragons.

Tonglong turned to the Emperor. "Do you know what this is? You should recognize its unique shape."

"I do," the Emperor replied. "It is a key to the Forbidden City."

"Correct," Tonglong said. "I always knew that my mother had gone to great lengths to obtain it, but it wasn't until I connected her with that traitor Lei that I realized what she was up to. Lei killed HaiZhe, not me. I planned to keep him alive and set the final stages of my plan in motion months or even years from now. Thanks to my mother, things have been accelerated. You are now a puppet, and I am your master. The Forbidden City will soon be mine!"

"Psst! ShaoShu! Let's go!"

ShaoShu glanced at the doorway and saw Long standing off to the side with Xie balanced impossibly across his shoulders. ShaoShu opened his mouth to say something, but Long turned and disappeared, leaving nothing but a shadow.

ShaoShu looked at Tonglong; then he looked back at Long's receding shadow.

And he chased after it.

THE FIVE ANCESTORS

adventures continue in

Book 7 . . .

龍Dragon

Jeff Stone lives in the Midwest with his wife and two children and practices the martial arts daily. He has worked as a photographer, an editor, a maintenance man, a technical writer, a ballroom dance instructor, a concert promoter, and a marketing director for companies that design schools, libraries, and skateboard parks. He began searching for his birth mother when he was eighteen and found her fifteen years later. He has subsequently found his birth father as well. He recently traveled to the Shaolin Temple in China and while there passed his black-belt test in Shaolin-do kung fu.